Jesus Trucking Company

a novel by
Rick Amidon

Halcyon Press, Ltd
www.halcyon-press.com

Published by Halcyon Press, Ltd. http://www.halcyon-press.com

All Rights Reserved

© Copyright 2001 Halcyon Press, Ltd.

For information, write:
Halcyon Press, Ltd.
6065 Hillcroft Suite 525
Houston, TX 77081

Printed in the United States of America

Library of Congress Cataloging-in-Publication Data

Amidon, Rick, 1959-
  Jesus trucking company / by Rick Amidon.
      p. cm.
  ISBN 0-9706054-4-7 (pbk. : alk. paper)
  1. Truck drivers--Fiction. I. Title.
  PS3601.M54 J4 2001
  813'.6--dc21

                                        2001000788

Acknowlegements

I would like to thank my wife, Denise, first reader, for her keen and intelligent eye and her many thoughtful suggestions in making this book better than it was. Also, to Chaz and Russ for, like Denise, enriching my life beyond measure.

Contents

1.	Planting the Children.	1
2.	Kansas	5
3.	Feeding the Hungry.	8
4.	Iowa	13
5.	City of Big Shoulders	17
6.	Woman with Two Hearts.	21
7.	Something Like Hope	24
8.	Saving.	28
9.	Chipping Away at Life	31
10.	Beneath the Bottom.	36
11.	Round Trip	42
12.	All That We Have.	45
13.	Letting Faith Go to Work	49
14.	Halves.	52
15.	Wanting to Get Closer.	57
16.	The Sudden Light	60
17.	The Hard Essential Landscape.	62
18.	Between Angels	66
19.	Just Outside Munising.	69
20.	Dancing With God	75
21.	These Roads, This Life	82
22.	Inside a Life	86
23.	Fall in June.	89
24.	The Arranged Hour.	91
25.	Going Back to Another Life	93
26.	Waist Deep in a New Life.	95
27.	Digging for Hope	99
28.	Reaching for Home.	102
29.	Choosing to Believe	105
30.	Parting the Reeds.	107
31.	Collecting	109
32.	Settling into the Earth	112
33.	Climbing Back, Climbing Out.	115
34.	The Idea of Seasons.	122
35.	Driving Home	130

For Him, of Course

Planting the Children

1.

He drives on.

Looking into the rearview mirror, Jack Cranberry's eyebrows wriggle like two impatient caterpillars taped to his forehead.

Along the South Dakota roadside, he sees withered billboards. Speed limit signs that bleed rust from bullet wounds. A disturbing message crudely scrawled on a distant water tower: "*Marge, come back.*"

He drives on, God's planet scrolling below the worn tires of his 18-wheeler, feathery wisps of clouds hanging above his cab like vaporous and poorly sketched haloes. The sky ahead looks no better, resembling the gray swirls of a sonogram. He slowly traces the smoky blurred lines with his finger pressed against the windshield, imagines he might locate a child in there somewhere.

His eyes are tired, bloodshot raisin eyes, even though last night he treated himself to a motel. Something he rarely does. Okay, so it was a Motel 6 in a bad neighborhood. Cheap, butter-yellow window shades glowed like perfect squares of English toffee. And the Gideon's was chained to the nightstand in his room. Still, Jack hoped for some rest.

In the room next to him, a young couple argued all night long, and Jack had to endure every word of it. Finally, at 5 a.m., they made peace and left for the Denny's next door, open 24 hours, for eggs, coffee, and closure. But by then Jack had written off any hope for sleep.

He was happy that they'd resolved things, even though they're lacking one very important ingredient in their marriage. The *main* ingredient.

The night develops into the darkest one Jack can remember. Ahead, he thinks he sees the troubling, throbbing lights of an ambulance, their brilliant flashers skewering the darkness. Jack feels a swell of panic, says a prayer beneath his breath. He likes it because it's one he made up. Easy to remember. It goes something like this:

"Heavenly Father, what I see before me just reminds us once again that You are in control, and we are not. Please have mercy on them. Amen."

Jack's eyes close for half a second, then reopen to find flares winking at him like old friends he hasn't seen in years. His eyes squint, work to see more of what he's seen on the road for years. Tragic accidents involving the young and the old. Beautiful people whose lives are altered forever, if not snuffed to premature conclusion. Jack comforts his heart by remembering Revelation 21:4, that one day *"there will be no more death or mourning or crying in pain."*

When his rig slows to a complete stop, Jack tunes his scanner to learn the details. Cars and trucks are so backlogged that drivers and passengers stand alongside their vehicles visiting with one another. Speculating the worst. A young boy points up ahead and tells his younger sister that there is trouble.

Thunder breaks overhead, followed by a flash of lightning. Jack thinks he sees mosquitoes separate into two different camps.

After an unsuccessful search on the crackling scanner, he

Planting the Children

jumps down from his cab and walks quickly toward the ambulances. There are two. A fire truck arrives at the scene before Jack can make his way through the chaos. The closer he gets, the more he believes he hears screaming; the desperate voice of a young woman, maybe in her mid-twenties. There is a police officer protecting the scene, keeping curious motorists at bay. But he says nothing as Jack trots by, as if he doesn't notice. Perhaps Jack has an official look about him.

When he arrives at the scene, Jack quickly realizes there is no windshield glass spread across the pavement like shattered hail. No car parts protruding from ditches. No bumpers and rearview mirrors and car doors propelled into the nearby field. Just an old white Chevy pickup truck, fully intact, sitting at the side of the road, the back hatch pulled down like a thirsty tongue, and two or three emergency medical technicians leaning into the rear of the truck's bed.

It is hot and humid and clouds of mosquitoes hover above the EMTs heads like word balloons filled with dotted static. A slight rain begins to fall.

Jack now stands directly behind them. The young woman is Native American, black eyes that appear to have been hole-punched in the middle of her thin, leathery face. Considering the geography, she could be Navajo or Hopi. Maybe Havasupai, but not likely. She pushes, screams in sheer agony, displaying slivers of rotten teeth. She is frightened and alone and determined and beautiful. More than anything, her pain traps Jack in the moment, narrowing his life to a series of crimson contractions. And he is just listening to it—not experiencing it as is the mom-to-be.

"You're doing just fine, Miss Smallbone," one of the men says. "Just fine indeed."

3

Planting the Children

Finally, she closes her eyes, purses her lips, and gives in to something larger than all of us, howling as her baby shunts along watersmooth walls, emerging wet and cold and gray.

This is the first time Jack has ever seen anyone being born. It reminds him of the time he was a kid, stopping on his way home from school to watch some huge bulldozer pull tree stumps from the earth, wet yellow clay dripping from its roots like butterscotch from a spoon.

Birth is like that, but without the butterscotch.

Facing away from the scene, Jack offers a word of thanks and praise to God for this new life. It is no accident after all. It never is when someone is born. Where and when seem like a mystery to us. But it is no mystery to Him. None of it is.

Jack takes a quick step toward the small crowd of three. The mother, exhausted but happy, says only "Mikumwesak." Though Jack has never studied or spoken this language, he understands that this is Abenaki for "little person."

"Do you mind if I lead us in a short prayer?" Jack offers. The rain now falls in sheets, its lines sharp against his weary face. The police officer steps into a puddle and an oily film parts in loops around his boot, glistening like tinfoil. He joins Jack but keeps his hands in his pockets.

The young lady nods yes, her eyes swimmy, a satisfied smile on her now pale face. Her baby wails inconsolably.

All bow their heads in prayer, even the officer, as Jack thanks God for this day, for this new mother, for this new child. He prays for their safety. To the east, a slice of moon begins to rise like a half-eaten holy wafer. When Jack concludes, everyone says "*Amen*" together, as if this has been rehearsed.

"In the same way, any of you who does not give up
everything he has cannot be my disciple. "

—*Luke 14:33*

In some ways his fall was predictable, though he certainly didn't invite it.

Jack hauls through Kansas, a garrison of windmills and small farmhouses greeting him at every mile. He notices a handmade yard sign announcing that someone named Yob is running for County Drain Commissioner. The entire side of a red barn advertises *"Suzantiques"*, next left. And a man drives the widest combine he's ever seen down the middle of the road. Jack notices the man bouncing rhythmically beneath a small black canopy, as if he's keeping beat with the earth he's about to churn.

Slowing down, recognizing there is no way to pass him and still be on the road, Jack decides to stop. Allow the farmer to get some distance from him. Perhaps he'll turn off the road and onto a patch of field.

Jack lowers the visor to reveal his aging face. Unshaven, he looks older than he feels. He is long overdue for a haircut, and he pushes his long fingers through the steel gray waves of hair. His own face looks bony to him, refugee-like. It occurs to him how his appetite has never been the same since he lost all his money. Years later, just thinking that thought—*since he lost all his money*—still sobers him. How could it have all gotten away from him, and so quickly?

One day he was wearing Armani suits made in Italy. The next day he was in jeans, wondering what the market was for used

5

Italian suits. The Salvation Army didn't have a history of *buying* people's second-hand clothes. They got them free. *Needed* them free.

But yet, years later, Jack is eternally grateful for his fall. Without doubt, he counts it all joy, a joy which weakens him in the belly. Brings small drops of tears to his tired eyes. Finds peace in the new man he's become.

Still peering into his tiny mirror, his eyes transforming like small vials of water clouded by red dye, Jack is startled by the blasting horn.

Behind him, without his knowing, an old El Camino has pulled up. The driver wears a cowboy hat and walks up to Jack's window, signals him to unroll. Jack obeys.

"You okay, Cowboy?" he asks Jack.

Getting his composure, Jack isn't sure of how he is to answer this question—and still be honest. Jack knows the man can see he's been crying.

"I'm just not feeling too well at the moment," Jack admits. "Plus, that combine up there. I was waiting. . ."

But the combine is nowhere in sight.

"Combine?" the man asks, looking quizzically at Jack.

Jack studies the road before him, finds nothing. "Yes. There was this . . . very large tractor. It took up the whole road. It was black. I couldn't get around . . ."

The man in the cowboy hat smiles. Jack notices how soft his eyes are.

"That was probably old Raynard Nelson, out for a Sunday drive."

"On Saturday?" Jack asks.

"Today's Sunday, Son. You got your days confused."

It occurs to Jack that the man in the cowboy hat is correct. How could he have lost a day?

"So, you're okay to drive?" he asks Jack once more.

"Sure," he answers, not confident. "Sure I am."

The man in the cowboy hat offers Jack his right hand. He accepts it, reluctantly. The man then gives more of a squeeze than a shake. "Just remember one thing, Son: by His wounds we are healed."

The man in the cowboy hat smiles once more at Jack, gently pulling back his arm, and ducks back into his El Camino. He pulls up, waves, and drives slowly on ahead. On the tailgate of the man's truck are the words **"Jesus Trucking Company."**

Feeding the Hungry

3.

"Simon Peter climbed aboard and dragged the net ashore.
It was full of large fish, 153, but even with so many the net
was not torn. Jesus said to them, 'Come and have breakfast.'"
—*John 21:11-12*

"Will it be eggs and bacon this morning?" she asks.

"I'm afraid not." The man answers her with quiet indifference. His big yellow Ryder idles outsides, a churlish hum that could be an old man's constant snore. "Not very hungry this morning, for some reason."

The thin man in the Peterbilt hat stands at the end of the aisle. He is surrounded by racks of granola bars and Chiclets, boxes of Snickers and Baby Ruths and Certs of every color, for every occasion. Skoal and Copenhagen displays compete with each other for the finite smokeless chewing tobacco dollar.

The man counts his lottery tickets, his long thumbs and forefingers rolling through endless strips as if he is the Postmaster General, dolling out swathes of new edition stamps to eager letter writers.

"You gotta have a winner in there somewhere, George," the clerk announces as she rings up another customer. He, too, requests a throng of daily picks.

"When I was young, I loved to fish," George answers, making eye contact only with his tickets. "You'd sit there in your small fishing boat for hours and hours, not knowing when or where they'd strike. Finally, you'd get a bite. What a feeling. Nothing was more satisfying. Playing the lottery is a lot like that."

In his travels, Jack commonly sees people buying lottery tickets at stores like this across the country. Over the course of a single year, some truckers spend more on tickets than on their loved ones for Christmas. The odds of winning a payoff in one state Jack drove through recently were 1 in 54,979,155. And yet, there was a line at the counter to pick that lucky number.

Jack notes that if there is one thing he's learned over time, it is that desire blossoms into obsession, envy into malice, and greed into rage. Very few happy lottery winners live happy lottery lives.

"When was the last time you had a bite, George?" a man sipping coffee near the magazine rack asks.

"It's been a long, long while," George confesses. "But even longer since I caught a fish." His audience laughs.

Once counted, George begins to scratch the grayish ash off the tickets with an old Indian head nickel.

Not wishing to intrude, Jack takes a chance. He introduces himself, asks for directions. Small talk, something he's had to work at.

"What do you suppose the odds are of actually winning?" Jack asks.

George pauses just long enough to offer him a wordless glare.

"I once tried to calculate the odds of a specific person—like yourself, for instance—being born," Jack says. "I spent a week doing this, mainly because I thought it would be an interesting challenge. Plus, it counted as work toward a statistics class I had to take once. I even enlisted some of the very best graduate students to assist me. Numbers-types. Digital whizzes. The math problem was not as easy as it appeared on the surface. First, you need to estimate the total number of men and women in the world. But not just *all* men and women, *fertile* men and women. For this I called upon the help of several urologists, gynecologists, and even the dean of the university's medical school. Then we calculated the number of different genetic possibilities a man might contribute to the mix, adjusted for the number of hours of female fertility each month, and then factored in a long list of other considerations. For help in this, I had to call on several faculty in the Human Genetics Department, Psychology Department, and even the Engineering Department. Not Human Engineering, but Mechanical, Industrial, and even Electrical Engineering. This was all getting a little complicated.

"This project drew out to one year and seven months. But, I finally got an answer. The bottom line of my lengthy calculation is that the chance of you, meaning *exactly* you, being born is 1 in 1.3 x 10 to the twenty-ninth power."

This impresses no one. A man sitting at the diner stabs at a slice of ham on his plate.

Gathering that they don't have a clue as to what his math translates to, Jack offers to help. He grabs a long piece of spent cash register tape from the open trash can.

"Basically, the odds of you, I mean *you*, being born are one in 130,000,000,000,000,000,000,000,000,000."

Jack writes this number out, complete with all the zeros on the paper trail. George looks up from his ticket rubbing, reads the numbers to himself.

"Yes, those are zeros. Twenty-eight of them."

Now George appears slightly impressed.

"We are not *lucky* to be born," Jack informs them. "Luck has nothing to do with it. God has *everything* to do with it. If you think about it, George, your chances of winning the lottery in your state or even being elected president of the United States are greater in comparison to being born. In other words, because of His love for you, all of us have won the genetic lottery."

George is done rubbing. Jack reads from the expression on George's face that he is winless.

"Look in your shirt pockets," Jack tells them. The man drinking coffee coughs.

"What?"

"Go ahead, look into your pockets. Your shirt pockets."

They do, one by one, starting with George. Each person pulls out a string of tickets. After a moment of confusion, they hold them in their palms like pearls plucked from an oyster.

"Go ahead, try them," Jack advises.

Again, they pause and then follow Jack's order. Each ticket is a winner. They fall silent.

The men stare at Jack in either disbelief or contempt, he can't quite tell which. Jack strolls over to the counter and asks the clerk for tickets.

"How many, Sir?"

Jack studies her question. "153," he answers. "Please."

"Pardon me?"

"153 of them," Jack repeats.

"Excuse me, Sir, but you would like to buy 153 state lottery tickets?"

"Yes, Ma'am," Jack says. "I would like 153 state lottery tickets."

The clerk lets one side of her mouth curl higher than the other side, then doles out to Jack every ticket she has left. Coincidentally, there are 153 of them. The truckers stand, speechless. Jack distributes handfuls to each of them. They rub off the first three. Each is a winner. Two fives and a ten. They rub off three more. One $25 winner, a fifty, and a hundred.

They rub off all of the rest of the tickets, ash being chiseled everywhere. All of the 153 tickets are winners. The clerk wants to call management, the newspaper, or the police. She can't decide who first.

"You are alive," Jack tells them. "You are here. Gifts of God. Make the most of this by praising Him. This is more valuable than any fish."

They stand in line to redeem their winning tickets. The clerk is sure she doesn't have enough cash.

"So you should save your money," Jack says. "Don't buy lottery tickets. Besides, you already won a lottery more amazing than the kind humans could ever invent. And you have already been awarded a grand prize far richer than anything the State Lottery Commission has to offer."

They wait in line for the clerk to call management for more cash.

"I hope our paths cross again some time soon," George says to Jack. The others chuckle and agree.

As he leaves the truck stop, Jack hears the faint sounds of their voices, replaying what they just saw with amazement, then ordering breakfast with hunger in their voices.

Iowa

4.

"The people who live in darkness will see a great light;
on those living in the land of the shadow of death
a light has dawned."
—*Matthew 4:16*

Jack is now in Iowa, at a truck stop along I-80. This is a place called EAT, a simple diner where breakfast is served 24 hours a day. There is a rancid smell here that Jack can't quite place.

Outside, weeds push through sidewalk cracks like the fingers of curious thieves. Dead clutches of dandelions huddle in gnarled tufts. Two dozen cows dot a small meadow. A parked semibears the bumper sticker '*Cover me, I'm changing lanes,*' while another truck advises: '*Forget about world peace . . . visualize using your turn signal!*'

Inside, the atmosphere is crude; truckers and bikers recite four-letter words that haven't made it to the high schools yet. Tasteless and bawdy jokes about women abound, along with lewd tales that could never be even half-true.

The waitress is older, Jack notices. Coppery hair, high cheekbones, prairie wolf's eyes. She herself is the subject of several errant shots, launching murderous glances at her customers whenever they request more coffee. She notices Jack notice her, and so she glances over to the manager, a small bald man sitting at the cash register. Two bikers in black sit at the counter next to Jack and complain about her attitude. Her mood. Her rudeness. The way she seems to bore her green eyes right into you when you place your order. As if she dares you to offer a smile, or a friendly "Good Morning."

"No way could she lighten up," one of the bikers remarks,

13

"even if her life depended on it."

"Old Paula's bad to the bone," says the other. He lights, then waves a cigarette as if he was conducting the Boston Pops.

Jack wonders for a moment what her life is really like. For instance, outside the restaurant.

What was her home life like while growing up? Did she get enough education? Has she been married? Have her children become ill? Did she hold her mother's hand while she died in her arms? Has anyone ever bought her a cup of coffee?

"Miss," Jack says to her, softly.

"What'll it be today?" She is short with him, eyes downcast, ready to record Jack's order in diner shorthand.

Jack pauses. Finally, the words complete the tortuous journey to the tip of his tongue. "Do you have Jesus in your life?"

She looks up to him, stares into his kind eyes. She first nods yes, then no. A tiny tear forms in the rim of her red left eye. Jack imagines the bikers next to him, pausing mid-bite to watch, see what happens next. But he can't take his eyes off her. Suddenly, this 50-year-old woman who looks to have lived a terribly rough life becomes the most beautiful person in the world.

"He loves you," Jack assures her. He wishes he could state this more sagely, though he has practiced. Time and again he has rehearsed it, but it never comes out like he intends. But thanks to the Holy Spirit, it does get out . . . a small miracle in itself.

"Can you take a break?" Jack asks. "To talk . . . just talk." She is petrified and this makes him nervous. Scared, in fact. Jack doesn't know what to do next, what to say.

Even though he knows what her answer will be, the words Jack is about to hear still feel like a death sentence being pronounced on him.

"Sir, please order or I will have to call out the manager." Her tears evaporate, instantly, leaving her voice raspy, more pointed than ever. Her raw face suddenly hardens like drying plaster.

Jack looks helplessly around the restaurant, the paraphernalia of trucking filling every inch of it: Peterbilt hats. Red Man containers. Yesterday's newspapers flipped to the NASCAR results. Black and white photographs signed by Rusty Wallace and Jeff Gordon hang unevenly near the cash register, slightly below a frayed dollar bill pinned to the paneling.

"I apologize if I have . . . made you feel uncomfortable, Miss," Jack says, the thinness of his voice making it clear this isn't working out like he'd hoped. He tents his fingers, then clasps them.

"Don't let the door hit you, Mister."

She looks as if she's suddenly wounded him, perhaps with some blunt instrument.

"May I have more?"

"More?" she asks.

"Yes. More about you. So when I pray for you . . ."

Paula weighs his question, then lumbers over to grab her checkbook from her purse. She tears off a deposit slip and hands it to Jack. "There. It has my name, address, social security number, and phone number. Go ahead and pray your little heart away, Mister. Oh, and my bank account is listed right there." She points. "Feel free to make as many deposits as you'd like."

While Jack finishes his coffee, the two bikers next to him at the counter surprise Jack with their assertiveness. They discretely inform him that her name is Paula and that her twin sons are doing time in the Iowa State Penitentiary—for armed robbery.

"It's the most horrid prison in the Midwest, Man. There's one guy in there that was convicted of *accidentally* shooting a cop.

Iowa

Twelve times!" They laugh, revealing stained and bent teeth.

Jack then learns that Paula's husband's an alcoholic and disappeared years ago. Her only sister, Pearl, hanged herself in the family's basement when she was a teen, a home life so unbearable death seemed like the only way out.

"You're from around here," Jack says to the bikers, assuming they are locals.

"Man, no one is from around here. Everyone just passes through this place. We just know the story because every once in awhile when we stop she's in just the right hateful mood and she spills it all to whoever listens. Every detail."

Jack manages to thank them for sharing this, and he pays his bill.

He leaves Paula a tip, which is larger than the cost of the meal. Though he can't really afford it, he can't really afford not to. Need is scrawled all over her helpless face. Jack goes overboard thanking her and wishing her a good day, ensuring her that God is good though life is hard, his worried eyes at odds with his happy lips.

City of Big Shoulders

5.

"But if we walk in the light, as he is in the light, we have fellowship with one another, and the blood of Jesus, his Son, purifies us from sin."
—1 John 1:7

He has always wanted to do this.

For years Jack has thought about it. Been tempted. Today, though, for whatever reason, he finds the courage.

Jack drives through Chicago on the Dan Ryan and takes the Ohio Street Exit. Because he's from a small town, inner cities have always intimidated Jack. After his third orbit of downtown, he pulls over for directions. He's longed to visit this small Christian college, one he's heard about for years. Read about. Dreamed about.

The early morning windy city streets are glutted with purposeful traffic. Jack drives through a row of pawnshops, watches a man walk out from one with a chain saw. Ordinarily this would not surprise Jack, but he's in downtown Chicago. There's one tree every six square miles.

Once there, Jack is momentarily lost on campus when he is approached by a man offering directions. He is an employee of this particular college. Jack picks up on that because he wears a name badge that reads "Floyd." Floyd sports a clean, bluish, short-sleeved jumpsuit and a ball cap that states the name of his college. His eyes, nose, lips, and ears are thinly outlined in black as if he's been sketched first in charcoal and then water colored. Perhaps he was a chimney sweep in the original 'Mary Poppins.'

"I'm in boiler room ministry. The boiler died this morning," he says. "It's a dirty job, but someone's got to renew it."

17

Jack greets Floyd and asks him how he is. He proceeds to welcome Jack to campus. And before Jack can ask for directions, Floyd very pleasantly and professionally begins to tell Jack about his college's ministry. And then he states that not only does the college serve students so that they may become equipped to serve others in Christ, but that every employee of his college has his or her own personal ministry. He happens to have several.

"For instance," Floyd adds, "you probably think that I am a janitor. Well, yes, I do happen to do a lot of maintenance and housekeeping work through the course of my day. But I also have my own toilet ministry."

"Toilet ministry?" Jack repeats with great interest.

"That's right. Toilet ministry. To the dorm students that live on this campus, clean and sterile bathrooms are very important. And ones that work. Oh, they could still get by with dirty and germ-infested toilets, but if their toilets are sparkling clean and germ-free, then they don't have to worry. They can spend their time focusing on learning more about Christ so that they can serve as missionaries throughout the world."

Floyd is upbeat and very enthusiastic about his toilet ministry. His attitude is like that of a child who has mastered riding a bicycle for the first time.

"But that's not all," he adds. "I also have a shower ministry, a vacuum ministry, and a repair ministry."

"Repair ministry?"

"That's right," he says. "I repair boilers, obviously, but also air conditioners, running faucets, broken windows, you name it. Almost anything that gets broken around here, I fix. Me and my co-workers. Apostles of mine in the repair ministry. Together we're a team."

Jack is curious to learn if Floyd is a new employee, as he is so fired up. Surely this must be his first week. Perhaps today is coincidentally his first payday. Jack guesses maybe his first check in years.

"I've been here for 16 years and about 4 months, but that includes the 5 years that I was a student here."

"You're a graduate?" Jack asks, a little surprised, but trying not to offend Floyd.

"Oh yes. Some people think that janitors never went to college. Or even graduated from high school. But several of the repair ministry apostles have attended this or another fine college. We're not dumb people."

"I apologize to you if my question came out that way," Jack says, recovering. "Floyd," he adds quickly, trying to bail himself out. "It's been so nice to meet you. Your college should be very proud of you. By the way, can you tell me where the Student Union is?"

"And for what it's worth," he adds, "my job is important."

"I am sure it is."

"No, you don't seem to understand. My job is *very* important. As important as the big guy upstairs." Floyd points upward. Here, Jack is fairly certain Floyd refers to the college's president and not God.

"I don't doubt that for a moment," Jack says. "The Student Union?"

"Yes," he says, "no problem. But for that you would want to consult our map ministry."

Floyd pauses, looks over his right shoulder.

"And who would that be?" Jack asks, somewhat reluctantly.

19

"That would be me as well. You're awfully lucky I am in today."

Floyd produces a campus map from his back pocket, and proceeds to give Jack directions. He dips into his pocket and plucks out a *Sanford Pocket Accent Highlighter*, fluorescent yellow, to indicate the best way there. Jack wonders if Floyd ever worked for a Welcome Center.

"Thank you," Jack says, sincerely appreciating Floyd's act of kindness.

"My pleasure," Floyd answers. "Oh, and while you're there, at the Student Union. Check out the cappuccino ministry. It's awesome."

6.

"When Jesus heard that John had been put in prison,
he returned to Galilee."
—Matthew 4:12

Just after midnight on December 6, 1999, the State of Iowa announced its plans to execute twin brothers Jay and Ronnie Weller for their part in a brutal armed robbery and murder at a rural gas station and party store. The owners, an elderly couple, were killed in cold blood. The crimes were committed on a bitterly chilling night in 1982.

The death sentence awarded by the jury had been appealed several times. Protests have been constant. Paula Weller, their mother, wrestled with her emotions since that grim night nearly 20 years ago. Her husband, the twins' father, abandoned them when the boys were just kids.

How many more stays of execution were in the offing, no one but God knew.

Jack learns all this at the county seat, stopping on his way to research it all. He wants to rush back to the diner called EAT, hold Paula. Weep with her. Console her. Tell her something to ease the pain, mend the wounds. Share with her Matthew 4:12 through 16.

Jack withdraws her bank deposit slip from his billfold and stares at her vitals. Oh to be able to make a deposit into her account.

The courthouse clerk mentions to Jack that the execution is scheduled for a week from Monday. His eyes pulse in somber surprise. It's no wonder Paula is so bitter, Jack thinks. Imagine—to lose both your sons. At once. Like this. Worse, it's a small town and everyone knows your business. Shares it. Eats it for breakfast. Everyone knows Paula.

And everyone avoids her, especially her eyes, hardened by years of humiliation and pain. Devoid of any remnant of kindness, as if she can't remember even the procedure for smiling.

Outside the courthouse someone whistles and a stray dog freezes.

Another whistle and it retreats, casting resentful glares at Jack over its shoulder. He knows this stranger's not from around here.

Jack drives back to the diner. Indeed, Paula is working. This is her life.

At the counter an elderly trucker stares straight ahead, smoking a fresh Tiparillo. A tiny cloud wreaths his head.

Waylon Jennings sings a song on the radio that sounds like the Monday Night Football theme, but with lyrics that are different yet. But then aren't they always, each week, depending on the match up.

Other men eat their lunches and read their papers in silence, a congregation of socially impotent customers.

Jack stares at Paula for a long moment.

"Do you want some eggs, Mister?" she finally asks Jack. "If so, you need to take a seat first. We're not a drive-thru here."

In the kitchen, a young boy is taking lessons from the older bald man who was at the cash register last time Jack was in. They wear the same hairline so Jack assumes this is a father-son deal. Paula turns from Jack, fills a copper kettle from the sink and places it on the stove with all the care of a timid gardener. Blue flames wink from beneath the kettle.

"Listen, Paula," Jack begins. "I know your story. I know your name. I know about your sons and I want to help you."

"That's good to know," she deadpans, casting him a weak stare. After five seconds pass, she finally nods vaguely.

The men in the diner stare at the scene as if they are all part of the same mute jury.

"I would like to talk to them about Christ," Jack adds. "Before . . ." Words catch in his dry throat, but he somehow manages. "Before it is too late."

Paula stands behind the counter, closes her eyes, emotion creasing her hard face. "Okay," she says. "Okay."

"We fix our eyes not on what is seen, but on the unseen. For what is seen is temporary, but what is unseen is eternal."
—2 Corinthians 4:18

Jack dropped out of graduate school. While there, he studied accounting and finance. His roommate, Max, was a psych major. Jack studied numbers and Max studied Jack studying numbers.

Max was a professional college student, having taken every course the Psych Department offered—and aced each one of them. Some twice. He was the model graduate student. Academic looking, a thin vein on his temple that writhed like a bagged snake beneath his skin whenever he was deep in thought. He had published several articles and had a contract from a renowned New York publishing house to produce his dissertation which was on, in layperson's terms, *what makes people tick.*

Max was brilliant. His future was pretty much a sealed deal, as colleges and universities from around the country were recruiting Max to teach and research for them. After it became clear to Jack that grad school was not his *gift,* he acknowledged that his bachelor's degree in accounting was sufficient for his goals. So Jack slipped out of college but stayed in touch with Max.

Max got married and had a child, a son named Brent. He was 9.

One day after a rigorous study marathon in the university's library, Max returned to his family's apartment, changed into his Nike shorts and t-shirt, and went for a five-mile jog. Upon returning, he found his son Brent tooling around in the parking lot with his bicycle. Max was tired, stressed out from too many classes, and his entire body seared in pain from his workout. He felt as though me might be coming down with the flu, his muscles broken, as if shattering inside his body. All in all, Max was so focused on his own condition and on his own needs that he was oblivious to his own son Brent's.

"Don't ever grow old," Max whined to Brent, lamenting over his own aches and pains. A calf muscle bounced, nervously, a stress-related twitch. He claimed it felt like a battery, implanted beneath his skin, that oozed hot alkaline.

That afternoon while Max was showering, his son's bike was clipped in the parking lot by another tenant. The driver had been drinking, having stopped on her way home from work to a happy hour with her staff. It was Friday, time to let loose. Relax. Let your hair down. Help the gin industry a bit. Little Brent was killed on the spot.

Max blamed his son's death on God. And himself for wishing his son would never grow old.

Still today Jack tries over the phone to explain to his ex-roommate Max that our earthly bodies are frail. At best. Clay pots, easily fractured and broken. That the Bible compares us to a tent, flimsy, needing only to be struck by a barley cake and it will collapse.

"The Bible isn't even good fiction," Max retorts.

Jack tries his hardest to witness to him.

But he only laughs at Jack's faith.

"Faith," he cracks, cynically, "what is it . . . what could it be . . ."

Jack tells him. "It's . . . faith is believing in the Word of God. And then doing what the Word says, regardless of your feel-

25

ings."

"Why?"

"Because . . . because God has promised a good result."

"Look," he says, pointing to a cloud formation. "I think I spot the president of the United States. Or no, maybe it's an animal—a Golden Retriever with sunglasses creeping under a white picket fence. And there's a Gateway computer monitor, a VX900. Oh, and over here is the State of Florida. And this knot on this big oak tree? That's Saint Paul. Or is that Saul? I spilled my orange Gatorade after my jog last night. At first I thought I'd made a mess, and in the right light, I saw a Renoir. So I'm famous. I'm rich. That's faith. Imagination. Delusion. Self-deception. Playing tricks on yourself in order to survive this life."

He contorts his face, tries to express falsified awe.

Today Jack visits Max in his Montana trailer.

He holds his friend in his arms, until he weeps. He smells like gasoline. His shirt and slacks have been doused. Years following his son's tragic death, he is a cynical man with a plan who only needs to be ignited.

"There's a hole in the world where light comes in," he says, taking a sharp breath, summoning more words from some deep verbal well. "It's accidental. Not part of any grand plan. There's no such thing as God. No such thing as faith. Do you hear me?"

Jack walks with him, carries him to the local hospital emergency room. To get help. To heal. To recover. To trust.

"I think . . ." he begins as he is waiting to get treated, but he stops there, not knowing the end of the sentence.

Max still blames Him for what happened to his son, Brent. Jack has been trying to help Max change his heart ever since. He informs Max that God had *little* to do with his son's death. And that the drunken driver had *everything* to do with his son's death. And though Max understands psychology, he doesn't have a clue about what really makes people tick.

Saving

8.

*" . . . always be prepared to give an answer to everyone who
asks you to give the reason for the hope that you have."*
—1 Peter 3:15

Paula's eyes mist over.

Jack sits with her across from the twins. There is a window
between the two couples, and Paula holds their hands through the
small opening. She wears a weary, defeated look on her face, man-
aging an occasional sad smile in between words.

She blinks black tears, her mascara spreading like the sad
eyes of a depressed raccoon.

The twins stare at Jack as if he is an alien. Which, to them,
he is.

"And Jesus said," Jack concludes, "I am the way and the
truth and the life. No one comes to the Father except through me."
Jack shares this with them *after* they said it. After all *three of them*
said it. Said *yes*. Said *I do*. And Jack believes they meant it in their
hearts. Of course, this is just Jack's opinion. He is not the real
judge.

The question, of course, was "Do you accept Him as your
personal savior? And do you repent of your sins—everyone of
them, big and small."

Later, in the attorney's office, Jack and Paula wait in
silence, sipping cold coffee. A large man with a shock of white hair
and small eyes sits across from them in the waiting room. Though
he is well dressed, he sits in a wheelchair. His large corpselike
arms hang stiffly at his sides. Jack's hope this afternoon is to enlist
her lawyer's help in getting one more stay of execution. Just one
more. So that the twins can be baptized. It could be done as early

as tomorrow. Or later today, possibly.

This story is headline news, locally and nationally. The governor is involved.

"My heart goes out to you, Miss," the large man says. His voice fills the small room. "I've been following your story."

Paula is still and stares straight ahead.

"Thank you, Sir," Jack responds.

The large man in the wheelchair takes a deep Perry Mason breath. "If you'd like my two cents, I'd bribe some forensic pathologist. You know, to complicate things. Hang a jury. One can be bought. Trust me, money fixes all things. This world is made of lies. Find or buy some good ones, Miss, that's my two cents. Me, I have led a dishonest, corrupt life. I came by wealth in an unenviable way. Started casinos in Michigan. Loaned seed money to the tribes, at 26 percent interest. That was only the beginning. The rest is rather boring by my account. I do happen to have more legal problems than the last three presidents combined. I know you're here to see your attorney. He's one man working on your case. I have a staff of them working for me."

Jack smiles, thinks he's trying to be at least a little funny.

"Let me just tell you what I own, if you don't mind. I own school buildings in New Jersey, private ones. Real estate in Miami, a soccer team in England, and even six cruise boats in the Caribbean. Never been on a one of them. I hate the water if you want to know the truth."

He coughs heartily, then continues.

"I'm old, I'm sick, and I am eager to die. Why I'm not six feet under is a mystery to all who know me. All I can figure is that God won't let me die. That death is too good for someone like me. Living like this, in pain and misery, is more appropriate, more deserving, despair anchored in my soul like fat road kill. No sense of hope. No gladness. No peace."

Jack rises, slowly, offers to make him a cup of coffee. The man waives rejection.

"Why would I drink coffee? To stay awake more than I have to? For goodness sake." Again, the laugh.

"Why," Jack asks, "or maybe how . . . *how* can you be so miserable, Sir?"

Paula's eyes, long immune to unhappy people, carefully, strategically go to him as he speaks.

"Where would I begin. As I told you, I am wealthy. Very wealthy. But dying. I'm told by doctors that tumors bubble in me like hot geysers at Yellowstone. I'm dying and am eager to do so, like I said. I have high blood pressure. I lost my right leg to diabetes, and this wheelchair I sit in rolls on Satan's wheels. For the life of me I cannot figure out why God spares me. Look at me. I'm filthy, ugly rich. I'm surrounded by more luxury than I can ever comprehend. But if the truth be known, I have been miserable and lonely and bored with my unthinkable wealth. Completely worthless."

Jack feels so badly for the man that he crosses the small room in four steps and sits next to him. Jack places his hand over the man's. The old man pulls away violently.

"You, Miss," he directs to Paula. "You're here to get help from the lawyers to keep your kids alive. Me, I'm here to get help from the lawyers to get my kids out of my will."

*"This is the message you heard from the beginning.
We should love one another"*
—1 John 3:11

The sun is fixed in the Colorado sky like some interrogating lamp.

Jack thinks how some parts of inner city Denver look like some sort of medieval encampment, small trash can fires smoldering, two grown men standing over them, cooking hotdogs like ghetto chefs tending to the fine details before a gourmet dinner. He decided some time ago to get off the main interstate in this, his last year of driving long distance.

It doesn't take Jack long to figure out that he's in one of the most disadvantaged neighborhoods of the city. His route is hemmed by graffiti-marred buildings and chain-link fences. Shadows seep into gaps amid housing projects. Jack slows to a near stop as a basketball game is being played in the middle of the street. The players ignore him. Suddenly one of them jumps in front of Jack's rig. He slams on the brakes and thinks this just might be this guy's idea of humor.

But he just stands there, a look of hate and pain in his face. He wears a denim jacket and is gap-toothed.

Jack then notices through his mirrors that his trailer is surrounded by the guy's friends. A few rocks bolt off the side of his trailer. Jack realizes that the plan here is to raid his inventory while he is stopped. Perhaps rob him. Maybe even worse. Briefly Jack wonders if this is being staged, like Channel 13's "Crime Busters", where people act out some unsolved crime and viewers call this

31

special 800 number to leave a tip that might lead to a conviction.

Outside Jack's right window, sitting on an old porch, a small girl adjusts hunks of cotton between her toes. She waves her toenail polish wand as if she's taming a lion, completely oblivious to the conflict.

They must have seen Jack's eyes from afar; he wouldn't gun it and crush the man who stopped him. Knew Jack wouldn't be up for a manslaughter charge, even if there were circumstances.

Jack is now worried, asks God for help. Then it occurs to him that He is in control here. He knows the outcome. Knew it years ago.

Jack thinks to call for help on his cellular, but changes his mind.

Instead he unlocks the driver's side door and hops down. His legs are weak as worms.

Twelve or thirteen teens approach Jack, surround his truck. The leader steps up to his face, confusion dancing across his brow. Jack notices how he limps, walks a little like a child getting used to crutches.

"You nuts, Mister?"

Not so far off a siren comes to life. Napping dogs look up in alarm, bark and prepare to give chase.

Though his nerves are being assaulted before they even touch him, and a faint fever pricks along the back of his neck, Jack does not feel threatened.

"Maybe, but I have always wanted to see downtown Denver. I have traveled back and forth across this country for 25 years, but I have never been to Denver. Or Salt Lake. Or Indianapolis, for that matter. I am retiring this year, so I thought to myself, 'If you don't see those great cities this year, then you will never see them.'"

Jack knows how thin his own beleaguered voice must sound to them, and how his own eyes must look like a small mammal's in search for food in the winter.

The leader looks briefly upward, as if he wants to be somewhere far away. A few others laugh heartily. The leader reaches into his jeans and removes a small handgun. Suddenly the realization begins to blossom in Jack's mind—you may die today.

"Hey, you're leakin', Dude," his friend to the side says, grinning with a shelf of perfect white teeth. Jack tries to guess what is behind his smile. He points to beneath Jack's truck. Sure enough, there is a glistening bruise of oil, looking like a spilled can of Coca-Cola.

"Today not your lucky day, Mister," the leader says with a big smile. His teeth are yellow, like an old woman's toenails.

His eyes are hard and merciless and he has the odor of an overtime shift.

In the near distance, a second siren falls in behind the first. Jack thinks how this moment is quickly progressing from bad to irretrievable.

Two other men are now also in his face.

"Today feels like a good day for someone to die," the shorter of the two proclaims, his palms facing forward. It is clear to Jack this is a gesture intended to suspend the drama, make him sweat. And it works.

"You see," says the larger man. He pauses for effect. Jack believes he has the largest chest he's ever seen on a human being. There is something calculating in his expression, something to fear. Streetlights pop on around Jack, shooting frail moonbeams that cut weak diagonals across the street and sidewalks.

Chipping Away at Life

It was wordlessly decided that the leader would now take charge.

Jack's eyes travel from the others back to him.

His stony resolve unsettles Jack to the point that he thinks how flashing Jesus at him will spell out the end. *Jack's* end. And suddenly he feels like Peter. And this hurts more than anything. More than any fear. More than any emotional warfare that at the moment rivets through Jack's heart. He loves Peter but hates that he denied knowing Him. Jack hates it worse that he didn't seem to learn *anything* from that.

To his far left, Jack hears the garage door to his trailer clashing upward like breaking jars against the side of a house.

"What I have can be yours," Jack informs the leader.

The leader frowns, his Fubu hat resting on his head like a bottle cap that isn't twisted all the way on.

His twitching fingers are bony around the gun's handle.

"You got it man," he says. "Everything you got be ours."

"Willie!" someone yells from the back of Jack's truck. "There ain't nothin' here!" There is a slight pause. "Nothin' here but a stupid can of red paint."

"Yea," states another. "And it's not even a brand name."

Jack hears the gallon thud against the inside wall of his trailer as someone chucks it as hard as he can. It rolls a moment like a toddler's bowling ball might, and then halts.

Willie's eyes narrow hatefully. "Man, you one poor dude."

Jack says a quick prayer, then swallows hard. Here goes. "I have Jesus. He is all I need. And like I said, what I have can be yours."

Willie shoots him a look that proves Jack should have kept quite. Should have pulled a Peter. Should have given into panic

34

"Willie," Jack solemnly adds. He sighs, not knowing what on earth else to say.

Willie nods, as if some deep truth has just been shared. "You got it, Man," he says, darkly. "You got it."

"Let me help you, Son."

Willie steps backward, tries to maintain a counterfeit level of threat. "Man, just tell me, if you don't haul nothin' in this here truck, what you doin'? Nothing to deliver. Never hear of such craziness. Or are you like deliverin' me? Tryin' to save me? Is that what this is all 'bout, you riskin' your neck like this?"

The crowd backs away from Jack's trailer and he watches as they depart toward a neighborhood Laundromat. After they all dispatch, Willie offers a gaze with added intensity. "Enjoy Denver," he says softly. He then offers Jack his pistol. Jack hesitates, but takes it. "Ain't worth nothin' anyway," he adds.

And Willie walks away, slowly, slipping his hands in his pockets. He adjusts his cap. "By the way," he turns and adds. "On the subject of Jesus. I can relate. I mean, He's cool. If that's what we're both talkin' about. He da man, all right. And I suppose you the disciple. You drivin' yo truck around Denver with nothin' in it but some paint. You oughta use that paint and say '*Jesus*' on the side of your hauler. Or maybe '*Jesus Trucking*', or somethin' like that. Make your point lots quicker. Wouldn't have to go through all this business first. Just get it out in the open, be better for everyone. You understand what I'm sayin'?"

"Yes, Willie, I do." Jack smiles, relieved yet thankful.

Willie's limp disappears just before he turns a corner and Jack notices how he walks more like a man.

Beneath the Bottom

10.

"Brothers, if someone is caught in a sin,
you who are spiritual should restore him gently."
—Galatians 6:1

In his cab, Jack silently says a prayer, from the heart. He thanks Him for having spared his life. Again. No way should Jack have survived this one. Except for Him, he had no hope.

He maneuvers his rig through the neighborhood, staring straight ahead as onlookers, curious as children in a pet store, watch Jack with awe. As if they expected a death scene. But instead they are surprised. No gunshots. No screams. No sirens, at least responding to the situation in which Jack finds himself.

Caught at a stoplight, a young lady waves to him, smiles. Jack turns. She barely wears a thing. Wearable art. Mustard sling-back pumps with gold-hoop earrings. She mouths something to Jack. He doubts it is *Have a nice day.* She measures Jack with her eye, gauges the odds of a sale. Somewhere between nil and non-existent, Jack wants to tell her. But not because he is strong; rather, because He is strong for him. In fact, Jack fully understands that just because he knows Jesus, he is not immune to temptation. To sin. To falling. In fact, he is as vulnerable as anyone. Perhaps more so than most. Jack has come to not even pretend anymore that he is safe from Satan. No one is.

As he pulls slowly ahead, Jack catches her face in his side view mirror, disappointment written all over her expression. Truckers are usually easy prey. A little time on their hands. Cash in their pockets. Loneliness in their hearts. Intimacy, even temporary, in their heads. What is it with you? she must be saying.

Jack's foot then drops heavily to the pedal and he presses, keeps pressing, as the lady, a lustrous world of sinful possibilities, recedes in his rearview mirror.

Darkness comes quickly once the sun dips behind the sheltering bowls of the Rocky Mountains. Thin, vaporous clouds swallow what little light the sky and stars have to offer.

Jack feels a little more relief as he sees the *exit* to the interstate. Nudging on it, he shoehorns himself into the stream of travelers, and as he blends in with throngs of other truckers the last time he was tempted—*truly* tempted—comes back to him.

It wasn't all that long ago. In fact, it was just before he sold everything—the house, the snowmobiles, the Cadillac, the boat, the recreational vehicles, the cottage up north, the personal watercraft, the timeshare in Panama Beach, and the list goes on. Jack was a serious candidate for senior partner in the accounting firm that would some day bear his name: *"Jackson, Howling, and Cranberry."* Jack had worked hard, year after year, preparing taxes for firms, large and small, and individuals, with means and without. His life had become ironically complex.

He kept a list of 11 phone numbers to reach his three best friends.

He e-mailed his associates who worked in the office next to his.

He talked several times a day to a client in England, but hadn't spoken to his next-door neighbor in two years.

Jack's accounting degree from the university had prepared him well, and so the MBA didn't matter. Besides, graduate degrees were for people like Max. Intellectual types. Academics. Jack was more interested in making money than in making tenure.

The shareholders were to vote the next week. Vote to make

Jack a partner. With stock. With all the perks. With all the privileges. With all the toys.

It was near the end of tax season. She was Jack's colleague, at least for the three years she had worked for the firm, specializing in tax law. Jack was into investments. Tax Law was into slighting the government of every cent she could, legally. Jack was single, no problems. Tax Law was married, no children. Jack was focused only on his career, and exceptional at it. She had narrow shoulders and a flashy smile. She wore large Turquoise jewelry on every finger and each thumb. It was mid-April, and warm, a multicolored scarf that carried her perfume, advertising that Tax Law was either coming or going.

She had strolled into Jack's office just after lunch, announcing that she was tired and lonely, her eyes reddened with fatigue. With emotion. She asked if she could close his door, talk a moment. The hidden grammar of office politics all over her face. Of course Jack said yes.

It is all so clear to him, even today.

"He doesn't pay attention to me," Tax Law told Jack. *He* was her husband, a history teacher at a local high school.

"I am sorry to hear that," Jack told her, strangely unsettled, wanting to give her encouragement, perhaps a small, meaningless hug. Is there such a thing, he wondered at the time.

"All he is interested in is old things, history things," Tax Law said after a moment, moving over to Jack's library. Her polite smile wavered for an instant, eventually settling into something more businesslike. She continued to criticize History, how he found passion in teaching and in researching and in just about everything else in the world. But how he cruised through the motions when it came to her.

It occurred to Jack then that this story is nothing new. It'd been told a million different times, a million different ways. Sure there were subtle differences, minor variations, nuances. There always are. But essentially nothing else was new. Except that Jack had never heard it before. Like this. With someone as attractive and lonely and desperate for attention as Tax Law.

"I need affection," she then said, smiling conspiratorially, moving closer to him. Jack stood at his desk, shooting her a look of compassion. Of caring. Of understanding. But something in the way she wept made him wonder if she was someone with one too many secrets in her life already. Could the next few minutes result in one more.

Jack's dark eyes grew nervous and alert, like a raccoon's caught in the glare of unexpected headlights. He wanted to call History on the phone, immediately, get him over here to listen to his own wife. Get him over here to get a clue. But he didn't. Instead he wrapped a gentle, consoling arm around her shoulder, shuddered a bit as the silk of Tax Law's scarf and blouse brushed against his wrist, and he said to her, "You need to tell him this."

"You must be joking," Tax Law replied.

"Well, no," Jack said, taking a breath. Here, his mind reeling, dizzy, wanting only to escape. He smiled feebly, though surprised at how deeply her words pleased him.

"I need you," she then said, directly, signaling with her eyes toward Jack's brown leather couch. She seemed giddy, like the child who was permitted to stay up too late.

"What?" Jack replied, not blandly.

"It's you, someone who listens. I mean really listens to me. Someone who is . . . successful. I mean, look around you. See what you've done, already. I mean in your career." Tax Law turned toward Jack, her green eyes settling squarely on him, brushing from his forehead to his chest.

Jack raised the first two fingers of each hand to her soft, pale cheeks and wriggled them. "I'm sorry, but this is not a very good idea." He was powered by his resolve to settle this matter quickly.

Tax Law looked from Jack to the Persian rug beneath her cobalt blue high heels. She then took a deep, controlling breath and turned away from him.

Just keep walking, Jack told himself. And she did. Out of Jack's office. And toward the senior partner's office.

A week later Jack was working at his desk, unable to concentrate. A six-page fax came, the guillotine falling on the waxy sheets just before they sailed down to his plush carpeting, notifying Jack of his fate. First, a quick burst of paranoia. Then his heart did a mad percussion number, and Jack's breath had lodged somewhere between his mouth and lungs, unmoving in his anxiety.

Even today the scene occasionally replays in Jack's mind like a poorly made television commercial. And as if to make matters worse, the photographs of his nieces and nephews on his desk stared at him, lined up like jury selection, when the papers were served. A queasy, clenching feeling twisted Jack's bowels as his eyes passed over words too horrible to even imagine. According to what he read, Tax Law was suing him for sexual harassment. And as he continued digesting the charges, Jack's breath began to come short, as if one lung had stopped functioning.

The media learned about this within the next hour. Stockholders were notified. Newspaper reporters arrived in the afternoon.

And by the next morning Jack was packing. He placed his

nieces and nephew into a box with care, studying their innocent, stationary faces. Tears ran halfway down his own face. He vowed to confront this, to fight it. To liquidate his assets, to tap into his pension fund if necessary.

And this is what sunk Jack.

She won. He lost.

And now, after so many years of sameness, Jack's life would be changing so much so fast.

The world, he thought, can get along without him just fine. No career prospects, no home, no money, nobody. And no concrete plan of what to do or where to go other than to wander out into traffic, go from there.

The last Jack knew as he prepared to leave town, Tax Law was promoted. Made a partner. History was, well, history, their divorce finalized shortly after she prevailed in court, claiming that the emotional stress caused by the incident with Jack Cranberry broke her marriage in two.

Round Trip

11.

"The harvest is plentiful
but the workers are few."
—Matthew 9:37

The next morning Jack awoke in a panic, his alarm clock failing to stir him. Hurriedly, he dressed, stuffed his passport and some clothes into his attaché case, and raced to the airport. Impulsively he booked a one-way flight south, to warmer climates, where he would drown his sorrows in rum along tropical, sandy beaches. He dreamed all night long of relaxing on Flight 531 to Jamaica, of starting life over.

Running through the airport terminal Jack felt as though he could be in a television commercial. Turning a hairpin corner, following arrows to Gate J-22, Jack slammed into a young man, his luggage exploding from the scene like an Alka-Seltzer instantly dissolving in a tall glass of water. Mindlessly, Jack crawled to his feet and loitered, awkwardly, for about two minutes while the young man gathered himself, got to his feet.

Jack was about to continue on his way, but the young man's face startled Jack. At first, Jack wondered irrationally if the collision had caused this mess, but logic quickly returned. Then Jack sprinted to the boarding area only to discover the plane had departed on time exactly two minutes ago. The airline clerk was both apologetic and sympathetic. If anyone looked as though he needed a vacation, it was Jack Cranberry.

Depressed and still dazed, Jack collapsed in a chair at the bar, cursing aloud the name of the airline who boasted their own efficiency on TV. He touched his forehead with the back of his hand and drew blood. At that moment the victim of Jack's careless hundred-yard dash approached him.

"Are you okay, Mister?" he asked Jack.

Jack looked up to find a short, bulbous looking man offering him a handkerchief for the blood. The circumference of the man's head was too large for his body and his eyes were set too far apart. He appeared to Jack to have Downs-Syndrome.

"I'm Sid," he said. "I'm sorry if I made you late."

Jack shook his head in utter frustration, saying nothing. He wanted more than anything to be on that plane, alone in his thoughts, relaxing in the clouds. Perhaps with two Extra-Strength Tylenol and a bottle of some kind.

"You look in trouble," Sid said to Jack, taking a seat next to him. Gently he placed his short, stubby arm around Jack's thick shoulder. "Sid will pray for you, Mister."

Once it occurred to Jack what was happening, he stood. "Sid?" he asked.

"Sid. Yes. My name is Sid. I'm low function, but I'm harmless."

Jack slowly backed away. "You're . . . a retard or something." And Jack hustled off toward long-term parking to find his car.

"I'll pray for you!" Sid called out after him. "Seriously!"

Jack had left the airport by the time he'd realized he left his attaché case at the bar near Gate J-22, in the seat next to the disfigured man named Sid. But there was no way Jack was about to return to look for it. He'd had enough stress for one day. The retard named Sid could keep his clothes and his passport. And he could definitely keep his prayers to himself, for all Jack cared. What a nightmare.

Jack was extremely hung over the next morning when he

stumbled to the end of his driveway for the newspaper. But he had to scan the '*Help Wanted*' section, start the tedious job of finding a job. He saw the newspaper headlines. Then he stared in disbelief. His eyes had great difficulty focusing. When they finally did, the words caused Jack to become physically ill, right there, beside his mailbox. Jack needed to sling his arm around the post in order to stand. The headlines read:

FLIGHT 531 CRASHES—NO ONE SURVIVES TRAGEDY!

"We live by faith, not by sight."
—*2 Corinthians 5:7*

Jack's teeth bit into his lip with unthinking brutality.
Not sure at all what to do.
Or where to go.
Jobless, futureless.
A college degree, yes, but also a very big black mark on his record.
Too old to go back to school. Too young to die.
Flight 531 still on his heart. *I should have been on that flight*, he told himself, again and again.
Any tranquility he'd had, any stability, now shattered by the sight of reality all around him. Jack's were the eyes of some roadside animal, lit by the headlights of a car out-of-control. He stared directly into them—unsure of what to see, eyes opaque, intent on getting out of the way. But should he split left? Or right? Or should he veer off into the same direction the car veers?
The self-perception of himself as victim endured for what seemed at the time forever. Burned into his mind. How do you forgive a world that treats you with shrewd contempt? Isn't there a Tax Law around every corner? Just waiting to hurry up and make you fall?
This was a funny day, Jack sleeping late because there was no decisive place to go. Bursts of rain were followed by short intervals of brilliant sunshine. There's irony even in the weather, he thought.
Jack went for the mail and felt both cold and warm currents

of air intermingling in subtle gusts. The mailman sat in his truck with a blank, purposeless glance, handing him a stack of bills. Jack envied both his freedom and his indifference. His expressionless brown eyes.

Inside, Jack opened his bills, paid them off immediately, leaving himself little more than prayer. He sold all of his prized possessions, his trophies of success—his JVC stereo system with DVD, his new Cadillac Deville, taupe frost color, and even his Lands' End white leather sofa—in order to pay off his VISA and MasterCards. What he couldn't sell he gave away, a handmade sign stabbed his front lawn, reading *"Free Stuff."* And what he couldn't give away he dropped off, anonymously, at the Goodwill or Salvation Army. He decided, however, against donating his old flannel shirts and eclectic ties, mostly Christmas gifts from demented co-workers and elderly aunts, considering that the needy had suffered enough.

When he was packed, his suitcase spread open on the bed, spread wide open, its gaping mouth hungering for more, and just before he walked out his door, Jack got down on his knees—first time since a child. He pinched at the bridge of his nose, not sure of where to begin, but hoping to see hope.

"Dear Lord Jesus Christ," Jack said, his voice small and unsure. His chest surged with fear and unknowing. He didn't know where to start. All he knew was that he didn't like himself. Even his best side was off-center, doing good deeds only to get a receipt, as if Heaven were like the IRS.

"My way doesn't work any more. Show me your way, Lord. *Please* show me yours." The tension in his face, the desire in his voice, and the gravity of his request caused Jack to bawl.

Though he felt like a no-hoper, Jack remained motionless in

prayer, his arms and legs and even neck heavy from restless, awkward sleep. No job to report to in the morning. He felt an uneasiness about something in his troubled heart. It took him awhile to figure out what it was. Finally, he put his finger on it. He began to hear it. The same words, over and over.

Trust who?

Trust *Him*.

How could Jack ever trust anyone again?

Because He's not *just* anyone.

Jack had heard that God so often chooses to work behind the scenes in any given situation. If so, he couldn't afford to make a decision on what to do, or where to go, based only on what he saw.

What drew Jack's eyes to the window was, at the time, a big mystery. But there it was. A cross. The thin pieces of molding that kept the small sheets of window glass in place formed, of all things, a cross. That's right, a cross.

And for the next few moments Jack prayed about *the* Cross. *His* Cross. How the Cross of Jesus Christ is such an extreme thing. But then again, God had to do an extreme thing to get us to follow Him.

It occurred to Jack as he studied the cross in the window that no way could he reap the benefits of *the* Cross without facing up to the sins that required Christ's journey and eventual death. Not just any sins. But *Jack's* sins.

So he repented.

Took the first step.

Confessed them all, big and small.

After a moment of prayer, of asking Him for forgiveness, of asking Him to help Jack trust Him, of inviting Him to be in charge,

All That We Have

Jack was lifted from his weary knees. He slowly walked to his car, his second car, a 1977 Mercury Monarch, won in a bet with a rich attorney friend over a Monday Night Football game. As often as Jack cleaned it, the car still felt dirty to him.

Once inside, he sat for ten minutes, beleaguered by his uncertain future. Then he drove off in some direction, wondering if this was how this trust thing worked, his blood pulsing with the possibilities of serving Him.

Letting Faith Go to Work
13.

"I can do everything through him who is my strength."
—Philippians 4:13

On his way out of town Jack noticed along the lonely highway a semi-truck for sale. A full pull. On the side of it was painted a phone number: 1-800-CALLHIM. Jack had never in his life driven a truck before. In fact, he hated loud noises and grease. His hands had never been truly dirty. But Jack called the number regardless, from a pay phone since he could no longer afford his cell phone's monthly charges.

Jack recalls the day was very windy. Snow flakes, fat as shreds of white cloth, cruised through the winter sky.

The man who answered agreed to meet him at the truck. Once there, the man said Jack looked familiar. Jack told the man who he was and the man immediately put two and two together. He'd read about Jack in the newspapers.

"Well, where do I begin," the owner of the truck asked himself aloud. "You're standing beside a 1983 International Truck Tractor with an 1850 Cargostar Automatic Transmission. She's got slightly over 326,000 miles on her, but they're mostly highway miles."

He paused and offered Jack a curious look. Then he asked Jack what he was planning to do with a truck. Jack was honest with him. He told the man he had no idea, but that something just compelled him to pull over to the side of the road, get the phone number, and call him.

"I don't know what you might be thinking about me," Jack told him, shrugging, but not wanting to go into himself. "I don't have much money anymore, but I am good to make payments."

A semi tornadoed by in the opposite direction.

The man hesitated. "I'm not here to judge you, Mister. I'm here to sell a truck I used to drive. It's a good truck. It helped me raise my family. Put three children through college. *Private* college, in Wheaton. A Bible one. It got me and my fruit around. Safely. Oh, it broke down. Plenty of times. But things always worked out. The fruit never spoiled. Never. I always joke that the truck didn't actually deliver me anywhere. *He* did. I just sat in the rig while He did all the delivering for me. For all this I am grateful. Not to the truck, but to the Lord for the truck."

This touched Jack. But he still didn't have enough money to pay cash for it. Nor for the fuel to keep it running. Unemployed, a loan was out of the question. And he had no idea what in the world he would be doing with the truck if he could manage getting the title and the keys.

"Well, thanks for showing it to me," Jack said, conceding that this was going nowhere.

The wind whipped violently, blowing a riot of white scraps over the truck's hood.

Jack noticed a sticker on the back of the trailer. *How's your praying?* Jack wasn't one hundred percent sure, but didn't those messages on semis usually say *How's my driving?*

"Mister," he then called to Jack as he walked away. His voice was going soft. "I don't know the truth about what happened with you and the lady. I mean sure, I read about it. Who didn't? Front page news around here." He swallowed hard and took a step forward. He climbed into the passenger side of the cab, pulled the title from the glove compartment, signed his name, and handed it and the keys to Jack. "Whether you are guilty or not, it's not my call. Nor the jury's. Just *His*." He pointed above. "Either way, I sometimes doubt whether God can use anyone greatly unless he's been deeply, deeply wounded first."

Jack held out his hands. The keys to the truck fell onto his fingers like hard rain.

"Strips them away," he added, somewhat expansively. "It appears that's what's happened to you."

He walked away. "Oh," he remembered, turning back toward Jack. "There's a full tank of gas. It ought to get you well on your way."

"On my way where?" Jack asked.

"I suspect you'll know when you get there."

And he was gone.

Jack stood there, alone, staring at the keys in his hand and at the truck by his side. A 1983 International Truck Tractor with an 1850 Cargostar Automatic Transmission, with 326,706 miles. But mostly highway ones.

The wind carried plumes of snow off the top of the trailer, and it looked as if the truck was smoking.

After a long while of indecision, Jack unlocked the cab door. As he unlatched it, a fragile pencil-length of snow fell from the edge of the trim onto his shoulder. The open door let the cab's light tumble out and cast Jack's silhouette on the white ground. He then levitated himself into the captain's chair and studied the dash controls, his eyes zeroing in on gauges and instruments. Jack shifted in his seat. Twice. This was like an airplane.

Jack licked the dry insides of his mouth, thinking, praying. And he wept in a joy he had never before known. For 20 minutes he wept, before he even knew if the thing had an engine.

Halves

14.

"My grace is sufficient for you, for my power is made perfect in weakness."
—2 Corinthians 12:9

And so today he drives on.

And on and on.

Even now he doesn't fully understand it. He accepts it, but he doesn't understand it all. Neither gift does he quite grasp—the gift of the truck, nor the unending gift of gasoline. The latter gift might just be a miracle.

Jack accepts the fact that, out of seemingly nowhere, when he had hit absolute rock bottom in his life, when he was weak and hopeless, someone he didn't even know gave his truck to him. So what if it has 326,000 miles on it. Jack didn't earn it. He didn't deserve it. Surely he couldn't afford it.

Yet today, years later, the truck still carries him.

It has a broken turn signal he can't afford to repair. Consequently, he doesn't make many left-hand turns. Certainly not in heavy traffic. Still, God has led Jack, and so far he has not been lost.

And then there's the gasoline. The man who gave Jack the gift said, 'Oh, there's a full tank. It ought to get you well on your way.'

Those were his last words to Jack. That was several years ago. And thousands of miles ago now. But the truck has never run out of fuel. The needle doesn't even teeter, frozen on FULL. This, Jack understands, is incomprehensible. Some would argue it's impossible. But Jack has proof on his odometer. And in the fact

52

that he's seen 30 different states, some several times now.

Other than the bottomless fuel tank, which Jack imagines works like a basket of fishes and loaves, constantly refilling on their own, the truck has little else in it. But for a small handsaw beneath the driver's seat, a CB radio, a can of red paint in the trailer, and a black book sitting beside him on the passenger side seat. A dark, leather-bound Bible whose inside cover reads:

Presented to Jack Cranberry
By Him

on the exact same day Jack found the truck. Or when *it* found Jack.

The Book's tassel is marked in Matthew. Matthew 28:18-20, to be exact. There, these words are underscored in purple ink:

Then Jesus came to them and said, "All authority in heaven and earth has been given to me. Therefore go and make disciples of all nations, baptizing them in the name of the Father and of the Son and of the Holy Spirit, and teaching them to obey everything I have commanded you. And surely I am with you always, to the very end of the age."

Today, Jack isn't on the road an hour when he spots the black hearse pulled over onto the freeway median. Two men in dark suits stumble in the late August heat, amid high white weeds, their hands waving at Jack, flailing, cutting the air into slices of low sky.

The hearse rests in the actual median, dust still forming small vaporous clouds around its Uniroyals. The emergency lights flicker in neurotic circles.

Halves

Jack pulls over. It takes him awhile to slow, negotiating the shoulder's gravel as if he's driven truck all his life.

As Jack steps down from his cab, one of the men crouches in a baseball catcher's squat, a human gargoyle in need of serious help.

"What can we be hearing?" he screams.

Jack asks him what is wrong.

They both attempt to explain, each stopping in the middle of their sentences until their eyes wander back into focus. But nothing makes sense to Jack.

"The body. We're transporting a body from the funeral home to this . . . this man's home town." They both signal to the wagon of the hearse, as if turning the show over to the corpse. "It's like 70 miles or so."

Short of breath, he cannot continue. So the other man helps.

"We're driving along and we start hearing him . . . his *voice*."

"Yea," says the other, eventually catching his breath. "At first we thought it was the radio, but it wasn't. To make sure we turned the control knob so hard to the left we broke it off." He offers it to Jack, who reluctantly accepts the black dial as if it's evidence in a murder trial. For the briefest of moments he thinks maybe it belongs sealed in a plastic zip lock bag.

"Believe us, Mister," adds his friend. "Please believe us."

It takes awhile for all this to register. The men claim to be hearing the deceased speak to them.

"That's right, from the back of the hearse. From inside the casket."

"At first I thought it was me," says the first. "You know, going crazy. I've been working a lot of hours. Two jobs. Working

54

at the Food Lion, and of course driving the hearse."

"But I heard him too," his friend adds quickly, his eyes glassy with unshed tears.

"What exactly did you hear?" Jack asks.

A long pause. They consult each other.

"At first he was saying something about wasting time. So much time. You know, his life."

"Did either of you know him?" Jack asks.

They both shake their heads no.

"And then," adds the second man, "he says that he knows how miserable our lives are. Get that? *Our* lives?"

"Are they?" Jack asks.

"That's beside the point," says the first. He has large wet spots the size of lily pads on steroids where his armpits are.

"He recently left his wife and kids," volunteers the second about his friend. "Sorry," he apologizes to him. "And me, I steal families blind." His friend glares at him. "Before we seal the caskets. I take the jewelry and watches and sometimes even the rings. If I can, you know, pry them off without too much trouble." He wipes his forehead with the back of his hand.

"Continue with what you heard," Jack requests.

"Well, he then said something like 'No matter how horrible your life is, how filled with failure your past is, God can still reach down into the middle of where you are, and, and . . .'"

"Yes?"

"And change you," his friend completes the sentence for him. "Change. He kept saying it. Change. Over and over."

They both begin crying, finally letting the tears spill.

"Then he asked me a question," continues the first. He waits until he gathers his thoughts. "He used my name. 'Bob', he

Halves

said, 'Bob—have you ever wondered why others around you are changing while you're not? While you're stuck? Just stuck?'"

"Yea," says the second, as if now just remembering this. "I heard him say it. Seriously I did."

"'Stuck in the rut of sameness,'" adds the first. "He phrased it just like that. 'Stuck in the rut of sameness.'"

"What did you tell him?" Jack asks the two men.

"Huh?" It is a chorus.

"I mean, how did you answer him?"

They both stare at Jack. "You're saying you believe all this stuff?"

Jack studies them. Clearly they are two desperate men in the midst of personal crises. Jack doesn't answer their question.

"Do you have any idea what this guy did for a living?" Jack asks.

"The deceased?"

"Yes, him."

"I think his obit said he was just a truck driver," answers the second.

"Yea," agrees the first. "He was just a trucker."

Jack gives them back the dial to their radio, and visits with them until they seem composed enough to get back into their wagon, continue on their way. Jack has never seen two men this young cry so hard in fear.

And before long Jack is on his way too.

Looking out his window the dark road before him seems to mirror the night sky, a great expanse of blackness interrupted by small hints of promising light.

Wanting to Get Closer
15.

"If the world hates you, keep in mind that it hated me first."
—John 15:18

Jack returns to Iowa. To the attorney's office. When he arrives, Paula is already there, sitting in her chair, a hateful look on her face. Today her coppery hair looks like steel wool. She touches her own heart with her left hand, closes her eyes, takes one deep breath after another. Jack notices a Day-Glo Band Aid on her ankle, as orange as a detour sign.

On the other side of the room is the white-haired man. He wears a blue nylon warm-up suit. Reebok, the jacket reads. As Jack takes his seat next to Paula, the old man mutters on his cell phone while reading a thick document, perhaps a draft of his revised last will and testament. He nods sagely with each page he flips.

"What a coincidence," Jack says, upbeat. "Here we are again. Just the three of us."

Neither Paula nor the old man acknowledges Jack. The old man hangs up on the person at the other end, without saying goodbye. Jack notices his cauliflower ear and concludes he's been on the line awhile.

"How are you today, Sir," Jack offers, wearing his best voice.

"Dying, but not fast enough," he broods. The thinness of his voice makes it clear he is preoccupied with his proofing. "And by the way, no preaching to me today, okay?"

This hits Jack like the sudden removal of a tumor from his chest.

"Sorry," he says. "Did I do or say something to offend you last time?"

The old man peers above his bifocals, and smiles at Jack. "You held my hand. I assumed you were either gay or trying to save me. And since only about ten percent of the male population falls within that first category, the odds of you being a Jesus freak seemed higher." His teeth are a gray boneyard of dental neglect.

Paula glances quickly to Jack for his response, a trapped-animal look in her eyes.

"You're correct, Sir. I was feeling for you. Bad for you. I felt your pain and hurt and hate and I just wanted you to know that even though we are strangers, we are both God's children. He made us because He loves us. And as you were telling me about your misery it occurred to me that the only possible solution to your troubles is Him."

"Him?"

A boyish thrill runs through Jack. "Yes, Him. Jesus. That if you were to come to know Him, how much he cares about you, and how little he cares about your wealth and possessions, that you might find relief. And some peace along the way."

The old man sits, tongue-tied. After five long seconds he backhands: "Young man, you need to know something about me. I hate my life and I hate that it keeps dragging on and on and on. And I hate all of my children, all 19 of them, because each one reminds me of one of the six wives that I also hate. I even hate the one kid I fathered and never even met, the product of a one-week affair with a Mexican migrant worker who couldn't even speak English. But more than any of this, I hate people like you. Christians. In all my misery at least I accept the truth. I've never met a Jesus-freak yet who had a truthful bone in his body."

58

His eyes suddenly grow lucid as they focus above Jack's head. A knot of attorneys enter the room, linger at the edges of his wheelchair, unwilling to interrupt. One of them ties a small, white bib around his neck and begins to feed him jumbo shrimp. He closes his eyes when one is brought to his mouth.

"Oh," he says to the obedient cluster of lawyers. "Remind me not to give any of my money to the damned churches either!"

They roll him into the elevator. Jack and Paula watch as it slowly swallows him up.

The Sudden Light

16.

Anyone, then, who knows the good he ought to do
and doesn't do it, sins."
—James 4:17

Iowa was never better than at this hour, light and shadow mingling in the trees, the court ruling one last stay of execution so that Jay and Ronnie can be baptized.

"I had given up hope," Paula confessed, "when I learned they'd been sentenced to death. I mean, when they were children, growing up, my only goal was that their lives would be better than the one I've lived."

Jack holds her eyes for a long, tearful moment.

Standing in the prison courtyard, a local pastor blesses a large bowl of water. He then gently takes Jay's head and guides it toward the bowl. The pastor says a short prayer, and he lifts Jay's head. The same with Ronnie.

A thought runs through Jack's mind but slows just long enough for him to catch it. Or for it to catch him. Paula. She's never been baptized. To have this opportunity before him, here and now, and for him not to take advantage of it would be a missed opportunity.

"You're next, Paula."

She smiles, shyly. "All right," she says in her most beleaguered voice. "I'll do it."

Surrounding the scene are the media, attorneys, and armed prison guards and officials. Waves of Iowa heat wash over the men in uniforms, plastic coffee stirrers dangling from their mouths like anorexic worms.

The Sudden Light

Paula is baptized, and when she returns to Jack, she buries her wet head into his shoulder. "I just keep thinking about that man. The rich one. What if . . ."

"What if he's right?" Jack finishes the question for her.

"Exactly."

"What if it's true that there aren't any problems money can't solve?"

Paula can't help herself. "I didn't know what poor was until someone brought the truth to my attention."

Jack squeezes her hand.

"Jesus is the one and only truth, Paula."

"Get rid of all moral filth and the evil that is so prevalent
and humbly accept the word planted in you, which can save you."
—James 1:21

Today, when Jack wakes, his heart is heavy.

For whatever reason, every so often he knows he's in for a difficult day. Usually it begins with a sleepless night, his conscience hard on him, regretting past mistakes and sins. And though he knows he's been forgiven much, it doesn't help. Nor does it help that Jack soon will be crossing the Mohave Desert. A few days ago he was in God's winter wonderland, trees and lakes and hills. Today he finds himself in a wasteland.

At first light Jack has coffee and eggs at a small diner called FOOD. While doing his morning devotionals, he can't get Paula off his mind. He wonders how she is doing. Jack prays for her, and for her sons Jay and Ronnie. Perhaps it is another prison nearby in this small Arizona hamlet that prompts Jack's thinking, his mood.

Following his devotionals, Jack's heavy heart is heavier yet, and he decides that if this day is to be a poor one, he will at least try to bring some glory to Him. Somehow, some way.

Jack gets a coffee to go and asks the cashier, a man with a distorted face, for directions to the prison. Jack's not exactly sure why God leads him there, but He does. Perhaps because there are many more Jays and Ronnies out there.

The cashier reluctantly motions to Jack. "This way a mile, that way for sixty-six more."

"Thank you," Jack says, somewhat confused.

"I used to work there," the cashier tells Jack. Then he signals to his face. "After this happened, I've never returned."

"Were you a guard?"

"Psychologist," he tells Jack. "Most of the inmates there are rapists. Brutal ones. You don't want anything to do with them."

It kills Jack to know his story. From psychologist to diner cashier. A line down his face. A nose that sits off center. An eye, his right, whose lid can't blink well.

"I'm hoping to help someone today," Jack tells him. He offers the cashier his hand in friendship. The cashier doesn't reciprocate.

"Who?" he asks, suspiciously.

"I'm not sure yet."

"Good luck," he says, then he smiles, sighs heavily. "I thought I could help too once. Went to college, got good grades. My older brother did the same thing those guys do, and when he was killed in prison I set out to try to help. Try to heal them through counseling. Fix them. But to fix them you need to study them. So I studied them, their problems, their fears, their motivators. All of it. My research took me back to Darwin, and before."

It occurs to Jack that this man is quite intelligent. He speaks in a monotone, no emotion whatsoever.

"What have you learned?" Jack asks.

"I learned there is no help for them."

"I don't understand."

He glances to his watch. The restaurant called FOOD is slow this morning. After a moment of deliberation, he decides to elaborate. "It's all about evolutionary psychology and Darwin's theory of natural selection. Man was created to reproduce. Woman to bear children. Both come from apes. There's no debate in my mind."

"And there's no God in this picture? In your theory?"

"No, of course not. That's a silly notion, anyway you look at it." He pauses, gauges Jack's reaction.

"Please, go on."

"It's also about competition. Man's aim is to father as many children as possible. Woman's goal is to compete against other women for the fittest provider. Bearing that child is an attempt, hear me—an *attempt* to seal a commitment. Simple as that. Education, careers, good meals as far as that goes—all of this is secondary. Diversions from the number one goal of man, and woman. To create a race."

"That's what this life is about?" Jack asks. He is graceful and kind in his challenge. "That's the purpose of life?"

"Essentially, yes. It's a race to make a race. Men in this prison and in prisons like this cannot compete successfully in the race to make a race. In the race for mates. For them, rape is the best strategy available."

Strategy? Jack cannot believe this conversation.

"This is Darwinian, of course. You know, evolution. Sex is not about power or control or affection as much as it's only about one's reproductive fitness."

"And love?" Jack asks.

"Love. No such thing. You see, I've worked with these people. I have known them. The impulse to assault is simply genetically determined. Before birth. There is nothing that can be done to cure it. It's not a disease. It is a natural condition. My brother *was* one. His genes are very close to mine, and though I don't cross the line, he did. Several times. Until he was finally convicted. Sentenced. Then killed by his peers."

"I'm sorry."

"Don't be sorry," the man replies. "Sorry doesn't cut it."

"If that's our purpose, to reproduce, that's all, why do men mostly assault and not women?"

"Oh, it happens. You just don't hear about it. But by and large, males have different reproductive priorities and strategies. That's all." He gives Jack a receipt for his breakfast. "Have a nice day out there on the road."

"Do you know anything about Jesus? Jesus Christ?"

He laughs. "Ah, the Son of God. Yes, I know all I need to know about the Son of God. The Son of God is very good for the economy. God is a vending machine. Pay some money, get some God. God on demand."

Jack is at a loss for words. It is obvious the man needs to return to work as a few truckers amble into the diner.

"Thank you for your insights," Jack tells him. "I will pray for your brother."

"Sam?" he laughs. "Pray for what? That he's not in hell? There is no hell. No heaven. He was born because a man reproduced with a woman, that's all. He flunked out of high school, ran a rum shop for a while, conducted séances, a scam, for money, and went to jail when the police finally caught up with him. He died at age 25 and went where all dead people go."

"And where would that be?"

"No where." He coughs into a soiled yellow handkerchief. He lights a cigarette. "No where," he repeats, and he pours coffee at the counter to a man in a John Deere hat and bib overalls.

"He has watched over your journey through this vast desert."
—*Deuteronomy 2:7*

Once again Jack makes the long, arid drive back across this desert. For the fifth time in his life. Each time tempted, but each time hoping to come across a lost and thirsty soul.

Tempted, because of the loneliness Jack feels. And how people try to capitalize on his loneliness. There is a small but colorful billboard 60 miles into Jack's route advertising nude models. Come experience '*love*', the message reads. Easy off, easy on.

Next Jack sees an ad for '*Desert Liquor*', ahead three miles. '*Discount Drink*' is also advertised, next exit. Not quite as many billboards as Wall Drug, but close.

'*Oriental Massage*', '*Movies for Men*', '*Cigarette Sale*', and the signs go on and on. No signs, however, for the prison.

Everything in the desert seems unpainted, weathered to a windburned gray. Except for the jazzy billboards that have Jack's mind whirling.

Though he hasn't had problems with any of these vices, they do tempt him. And Jack can't really explain it.

For a brief moment Jack blinks, thinks he spots the big black combine on the road again, before him, slowing him down. Jack reasons this must be a mirage, for when he opens his eyes it is gone.

Jack then reflects on the encounter he just left at the counter with the former prison psychologist. Jack pulls over at a small rest stop, one without running water or toilets. He hops diligently down from his cab, stretches. He walks into the desert, off the highway a good hundred yards.

Here, Jack kneels to pray among a few cacti. He prays for the psychologist. Jack feels for him. Weeps at the sadness of his situation. Of his emptiness. Jack thanks God for his salvation and for the strength to return to that man in the café and try again. Do a better job this time, rather than just listen to his theories. His broken philosophies, demented by terrible experiences.

Jack feels great pain through all this. In a sense, he takes on the cashier's pain. And Jack longs for Jesus. Jack asks for the strength and wisdom and perseverance not to give up.

And he prays for all who are like him.

He prays for the rich man in the wheelchair, who serves a god named Money, that his bitterness and hate would be converted into forgiveness and love.

Jack prays for Max, that he might come to know Jesus. Study His life for a while.

For Willie and for Tax Law and for all of the hurting people everywhere. That God would be their one and only painkiller.

At his feet a small snake appears, interrupting his prayer. It is colorful, black and green and a little red. Jack thinks how in a different world, snakes might not seem so evil. But in this one, in this world, they are.

In one fell swoop, Jack pulls the handgun from his jacket, the one the gang leader in Chicago gave him. Jack takes careful aim at the snake, gives it the count of three to slip, slide, or glide away. To do something. But it doesn't. When he pulls the trigger and nothing happens, Jack cracks the weapon open. He finds it has no shells. Jack pitches the gun at the snake, and this startles it, motivates it to slither into other lands.

After he closes his prayer, Jack walks back to his truck. No traffic in sight, he swings his rig around, forms a temporary arc in the highway, then full speed ahead. He stops at the first billboard. Jack reaches beneath his seat and removes a short, rusty handsaw. He found it once while searching for a map. And he goes to work.

Jack cuts down each wooden leg of the highway displays, watching the signs fall before him like large, awkward Goliaths.

After the final sign falls Jack is nearly back in town. Not far from the café. Where he will stop. Correct some things. Explain to the cashier that Satan has used sin to harden his heart. That Jack will love him as a brother. Pray with and for him. And even use words if it helps.

Just Outside Munising
19.

"Finally, all of you, live in harmony with one another;
be sympathetic, love as brothers,
be compassionate and humble."
—*1 Peter 3:8*

Sunday. Surrounded by pine, spruce, poplar and birch, today Jack is in Michigan's Upper Peninsula, hauling west on Highway 28. Out his passenger side window, Lake Superior speaks to him with a beckoning call. She is the bluest eye Jack knows.

Jack stops in a small Finnish town, and is drawn to the nearest white steeple. Since there is no one behind him, Jack is able to turn left into a small IGA parking lot. Outside the store another man in a wheelchair informs Jack that church is only two blocks away, but when he looks at his watch he sees it is nearly three in the afternoon and that services have long ago been over. He sits in the small gravel parking lot of this meager grocery store, his gnarled hands twisted around the Sunday Free Press. What is it with me and men in wheelchairs, Jack wonders. Everywhere he turns lately.

His legs are thin, veiled inside worn mining cargos. His feet angle off like a penguin's.

Jack asks him if he has some time for coffee.

"Well," he tells Jack, "what I really need is more than coffee. I need money or a job or something that counts. Coffee is easy to come by. Everyone's offering it. Unemployment agencies, social workers, churches. They're all the same. They act as if coffee is the solution to all your problems. To life's problems. I'm 58 years old, irreparably old. I have been crippled since I was 17, my

69

body crushed in a mining accident."

He glances to Jack's truck.

"Let's see," he adds, " you're just passing through, so you don't know these parts. The landscape is beautiful, but we people here are poor. We either work in the mines or we perish. Those are your options. All my family has done is mining, so naturally that was my plan. I wasn't on the job more than two days when the lid crashed. Too much pressure from the north end. Poor engineering, they said."

"I'm sorry," Jack says, offering himself a seat on a nearby curb.

"That's what they said. 'We're sorry.' Then they gave me a huge severance package. $1,500. That was in 1959. It sounded good at the time. I wasn't supposed to live this long. My doctor is amazed. He was around then, he's 72 now. He can't look me in the eye because I got him to promise me I wouldn't live beyond age 25. But here I am. Broken. Poor. Bitter. Still not awfully old. And no signs of dying."

"What can I do for you?" Jack asks.

"You? Do for me?" The man laughs the laugh of the insane. "Why, give me money, Son. I need money. I am wretchedly poor. I eat caterpillars and worms and bugs every so often. I am serious here, young man. I am not trying to be gross. I am only telling you how cruel God is to me. I used to be able to drop a line in the creek and catch a Rainbow every now and then, but I no longer have the strength in my arms to wheel myself to the creek. The brush is all overgrown and this here chair doesn't have four-wheel drive."

"What about family? You must have someone around to help?"

Again, the laugh. "You know, after about 15 years of listening to my bitterness and my cursing God, they all abandoned me. Which was part of my plan. Wouldn't you? My mom stuck in there the longest. I think I killed her. She wouldn't give up on me, kept telling me that this life is short. That the next one will be different for me. But I used to swear at her. Spit on her even. She would cry, but she always returned the next day with a sandwich or a piece of blackberry pie. And every time she would give me something I would take a small bite of it, spit it out, and tell her how horrible it tasted. Just to hurt her. Just to pass on my anger, have someone to share it with. The misery loves company thing. You see, what I didn't tell you is that when I was 17, just before the accident in the mine, I was a good athlete. I loved to run. Man did I love to run. I scored more touchdowns for my high school than anyone ever in the entire Upper Peninsula of this here lousy State of Michigan. Forty-seven touchdowns in fact. I recall every one. And I was in love with a young lady named Amy. Amy Koski, from Naubinway, down the road. She used to watch all my games. We were going to be married someday, as soon as I had mined enough to get a few paychecks under my belt."

"What happened to Amy?"

"Same as what happened to everyone else. I pushed her away. After the accident. She would come over, try to visit with me like we used to, still talk about our dreams together, about our wedding plans. Then I just snapped. I informed her how ugly she was, and how I didn't want anything to do with her. How I never really even liked her, let alone loved her. That it was all a dumb game. You see, I was doing her a favor. I didn't deserve her. I didn't deserve anyone. So I thought I was being kind by sending her on the road to find someone who could take care of her. Who could

71

hold her with his whole body. Someone with some future, with some money."

Here Jack wants to tell him about the man he met a few days earlier. The one also in a wheelchair, though much older. The man with millions of dollars to his name. An unbelievable listing of assets. The man who was a slave to money, but was equally unhappy.

Instead, Jack kneels by his side and takes him by the right hand.

He stares at Jack, a startled look on his face. "What are you doing, son?"

"I want to help you walk," Jack tells him.

"I don't need to walk now. I'm old. Money is what I need. I'm poor as bad dirt."

Jack helps him up from his wheelchair. Looks down to his feet and ankles while doing so, praying to see them become strong. Praying to see the man jump to his feet and begin to walk. Join Jack on his walk to church, even though it is late afternoon and service has been over for hours.

When nothing happens, Jack says to him, "I don't have money for you. But what I do have I give to you, Sir. Money's not what you need. Grace is. It's by God's good grace that you can be saved. But you first need something money can't buy. Faith. To accept Him. To give your life to Him. Your sins. Your past. Let Jesus walk for you. You can't afford to buy that, Sir. It's not even for sale. Nor is there anything you can do to earn it. It's a gift from God. No strings attached. Just . . . just take it. Accept it. And though it didn't cost you or me anything, never forget what it cost God. It cost Him the life of His son, Jesus."

The man stares at Jack, struggles to understand.

72

"If you accept this," Jack continues, "get up. Try to walk. But let Him do the work."

The crippled man holds on to Jack for dear life, fear etched across his face.

In the parking lot a crowd of people watch. One lady drops her half-gallon of milk, spilling it like liquid paper.

"Why does this surprise you?" Jack asks, to no one in particular.

Finally, when Jack realizes the man will not walk on his own, he replaces him in his chair. Jack feels like an utter failure, but then he also understands that he is not *Him.* Never has been, never will be. But still Jack yearns to help.

"Thank you," the man says.

"Pardon me?"

He weeps. "For helping me. Thank you."

Jack doesn't understand.

"I feel . . . stronger. Healed somehow." He lowers his head to his meager chest, as in prayer. "Not completely, but still. Healed." Finally he lifts his chin. "Do you mind?"

"Mind what?" Jack asks.

"Mind if I join you at that church?"

Those in the parking lot witness this and are at a loss for words.

"No, Sir. I would be honored."

"I mean, there's no way I'd ever be religious or anything like that. But I am curious."

"Curious?"

"Yes, curious. Curious to see what you'd be doing there with it closed and all, it being late afternoon."

Jack introduces himself to him. He shakes Jack's hand.

Just Outside Munising

The lady in the parking lot continues on her way, leaves her milk to spoil in the sunshine.

"So, what's in the truck?" he asks Jack as he steers his wheelchair toward the white steeple.

Jack tells him the truth. "Nothing."

"Nothing?"

"There used to be fruit."

"Fruit," he repeats. "Fruit makes me hungry just thinking about it."

Dancing With God
20.

"It is not the healthy who need a doctor, but the sick.
I have not come to call the righteous, but the sinners."
—Mark 2:17

In his cab this morning Jack's coffee seems to taste better than ever.

He is leaving Michigan's Upper Peninsula, a beautiful world not devoid of hurting people. He daydreams of someday the crippled man and the young lady, Amy, somehow reuniting.

The daydream is suddenly snapped by a mental picture of Paula.

Jack stops at a small gas station, notices that an attendant services his customers. Jack realizes how rare this is. The young man pumps gas, cleans the windshield, checks the oil. Visits with the driver about the weather and about the upcoming Packer season. Jack acknowledges he must either be in Wisconsin or extremely close.

The pay phone is out of order, so Jack asks the young man about options.

"Just use mine in the office," he tells Jack. He seems sincerely pleased to help.

"Thank you, but it's a long distance call. Very long."

"Leave something, then," he suggests. "Whatever seems right."

Ordinarily Jack would hop back into his cab, find another pay phone. But he senses he needs to talk to Paula right away. Jack didn't sleep well last night, as she was on his fatigued mind. And her sons. And the whole last day of their lives.

When Jack picks up the receiver there is no dial tone, two commas in an already over-punctuated morning. When the service attendant comes in to make change, he picks up the unit, slams it against the old desk on which it sits. He tests for a dial tone and there is success.

Before Paula answers at the diner, a wave of static snaps in Jack's ear like a cereal whose name he's forgotten. Seems there where three parts to the jingle. Then he hears her voice, thick through the racket. She asks Jack to hold. As he does, he notices the attendant's Wrangler jeans are on the verge of disintegration. Instantly this calls to mind Jay and Ronnie. How they look to Jack like Edgar Winter's twins. The denim was torn so widely that their thin, bony knees peaked through the fabric like a set of twin dog skulls. Displaced hippies, sitting across from Jack in the prison visitor commons. Him witnessing to them and their mother at the same time.

Jay and Ronnie confessing.

Jack recalls every word of it.

"Listen," he stopped them, mid-sentence, "you don't need to confess to me. Or to your mother, for that matter. Unless you would like."

"But we lied like dope fiends in court," Jay said. "And we still got put away."

Ronnie sat silently.

"Just confess in your heart," Jack explained. "Before Him."

"We was just not ourselves that night," Jay continued, following a small break. Next to him Ronnie began to cry. "We had often had the thought of, you know, scoring somewhere, just to help us out. Our jobs were min wage. Mom needed money all the time."

"Don't put guilt on me," Paula said. A lone tear trickled down her left cheek, cutting a path in her makeup. "I don't work 12-hour days to feel guilty at the end of them."

"No, Mom," Jay continued. "You're missing the point." He looked to either side of them, ensuring no one else was listening. "Ronnie and I felt . . . feel like we shoulda taken better care of you. When Dad fled. And we failed."

Paula began to weep.

She ran into the restroom. After a moment, Jack followed her to see if she was okay. She was crying uncontrollably, her chin resting on a toilet seat, as if at any moment an ophthalmologist would check the pressure of her pupils. Jack pulled her away, noticed the toilet was clogged with tumors of toilet paper, wads of visitor trash.

Jack held her head close to his chest.

Then someone set off an alarm, a gratuitous sound that nearly shook the blocked bathroom walls. Garrisons of guards stormed the entire facility, looking for the culprit. Jack and Paula broke apart as if it were them being electrocuted and not Paula's sons. Eventually an officer announced it was a false alarm, the curiosity of a six-year-old boy.

After the chaos, Jack escorted Paula back to her sons. Through the window he took a very good look at Ronnie. For the first time Jack noticed that he didn't look right, didn't look healthy. His eyes were red, and he wore a stringy gray goatee. He was still young.

"I did it," Ronnie said, finally, his voice base.

"Ronnie!" Jay snapped.

Ronnie studied Jay a moment, then turned back to Jack and Paula. His skin was the palest Jack had ever seen on a living human being. "I talked J.D. into this whole mess. I got him a little liquored earlier that evening, though he never took a lot of persuading." He wiped his nose. "We was having beer and we weren't all that lost to the world when I said, 'J.D., I am tired of being dirt poor. Let's take that store with the old couple.' At first he laughed, then I said 'No, J.D., I am serious.' Then the rest is history. I figured worst-case scenario, I will take the fall. It made sense since I got the . . . well, you know Mom."

Ronnie stopped dead in his tracks.

Jack looked to Paula. Then over to Jay. Finally back to Ronnie.

"Disease," Ronnie said. "So we're like livin' temporarily in another world as we park outside the store, walk inside as calm and cool as can be, like we're Clint Eastwood in a movie. Lookin' back, it all feels like a movie now. Well, the old couple was in there, just stocking shelves with cereal and oatmeal and the like and I said, 'Sorry about this, but my brother and I is here to take your money. It's nothing personal, we just need it more than you do.' He laughed at me, the old man did. Continued to stock his stupid Pop Tarts. And he called out to his wife. He said, 'Ruby, these here brothers say they're here to take our money. Say they need it more than us.' Then he laughed again. This time more so. Said he had no money, but would write us a check. Then old Ruby began to laugh at us too. It really hurt my feelings. Mine more than J.D.'s."

He turned to his brother and grimaced.

"Then, I just . . . pulled the trigger, I guess. And my brother freaked out. Two shots and it was over. I got the man."

"And I got the lady," Jay jumped in. "Got her right in the chest. Right side."

"Not true," Ronnie corrected. He said it in such a way Jack

knew it had to be the truth. "Brother never pulled."

"Ronnie!" Jay objected, then stopped himself in a loss for words.

"Then we noticed a small boy lookin' up from some pack of baseball cards or something," Ronnie continued. "He was sitting in the corner of the store, beneath a magazine rack. He was chubby and had a dirty face and was too young to be their kid unless he was a mistake. J.D. and me, we just stared at each other. Finally the kid started to cry but there was nothing coming out of his mouth. Brother and I just slowly backed out of the store, opening and closing the door with care, the whole thing like we was in a silent movie or something. Then I remember the cloud of red dust behind my car as we sped away. Again, I don't recall any sound."

Jay smiled in pain. Tears danced from the corners of his eyes like an on-side kick in a close football game.

"And we even forgot to take the money," Ronnie added, a thought which occurred to him for the very first time.

Jack and Paula were quiet in their own private thoughts. Jack reached under the window and cupped Ronnie's hands. They were scarred and his arms were tattooed. Jack tried for Jay's hand, but he subtly pulled it away. Then reconsidered.

"Guys," Jack began. "Bad things happen in this world. Some more horrible than others. This would be in that category."

"Why," Paula wailed, breaking down again. Her face was nestled in the crutch of her left arm. "Why . . ."

A tall man in a guard's uniform stepped up behind Jack and Paula, informing them that they had five more minutes. Though tall, he was almost as scrawny as Ronnie, but without the hair hanging down to the middle of his back. He held a Mountain Dew bottle, about an inch of green fluid sloshing around the bottom. Jack thought how it looked like the engine coolant he poured into his truck that morning before he picked up Paula.

The four of them suffered from his cold stares.

"Bad things happen," Jack repeated.

"But why?" Paula asked, again. "Why to us? Our family."

"Because of Satan. Because he manages this place." Jack surveyed the commons. "He manages this prison. This state. This country. And this world. And if you look for money to bring you peace of mind or security or whatever, you will be big time disappointed."

All four of them held hands, under the window. Jack knew he would see them at least one more time, but it didn't matter. He still wanted to touch the three of them.

"Someone once said, only love makes this trip worthwhile."

"Time's up," the tall guard informed them. A little spray of green liquid streamed from his mouth. He held a rolled magazine in the other hand. Jack then noticed that he held a large plug of chew in the corner of his mouth. That was the purpose of the pop bottle. He stood next to them, strumming his bone-thin thigh with the scrolled magazine. "Now," he said, a bland smile twisting from his lips. A little more tobacco slipped to the floor.

At his truck, Jack created the nerve to ask Paula what was wrong with her son Ronnie. After ten seconds passed she nodded vaguely, then she went soft. "AIDS," she declared. Jack held her, the fight fleeing from her completely. "It's just so much."

Jack comes to. He is holding the phone, wondering where Paula is. Listening closer he believes he now lost his connection completely.

The attendant is back to work, checking someone's alternator.

Jack sets the phone on its old black cradle, starts to walk out the door toward his rig. But the phone rings, mysteriously, catching him in mid-stride before he can cross through the door.

Jack answers the gas station's ringing phone, feeling some sort of obligation.

"Yes, I was wondering if you could tell me what time confession is." It is the throaty voice of an elderly woman.

Jack is thrown for a loss. He takes her name, phone number, and offers to have someone call her right back. He leaves the gas station attendant a dollar bill, as well as the note.

These Roads, This Life
21.

"I have told you these things, so that in me you may have peace. In this world you will have trouble. But take heart! I have overcome the world."
—John 16:33

On his way south, Jack is overwhelmed by the number of trucks and vans moving along the highway. They are everywhere, navigating people's lives from point A to point B. Scores of them berthed just outside the Shell. They bear plates from Ohio and Florida and California and just about every other state but Hawaii and Alaska. Even Wyoming.

At the Shell, Jack attempts to refuel, but the tank to his truck will take no more. It is full, still. Jack says a prayer of thanks for the miracle of diesel. He's not exactly sure what this fuel-thing is about—though he knows He is behind it all, at work in his life. Jack trusts Him completely. He doesn't have much money, less than fifty dollars to be exact. Not enough to fill his tank if he had to. Yet God works to make sure Jack can still travel. Amazing.

As he looks around Jack sees angry travelers everywhere. The outrageously high price of gas, over $2.00 a gallon. And they're moving, many of them, so they have no choice. They must travel.

Moving.

Jack wonders why we must move so often. Job changes, relationship changes, climate changes, for instance. It comes back to Jack, reality. It seems as though it has been forever since he's been a part of the *real* world, whatever that is. Ever since the incident with Tax Law. Ever since his life was forced to change.

These Roads, This Life

At the counter, two young boys buy juice, some candy, and baseball trading cards. One of them rejoices as he claims a single card might be worth $40. The other becomes jealous and upset over his friend's joy. This is the real world. The mother expresses grief with both. Citing the price of gasoline, she asks her son how many miles per gallon she can get from those trading cards.

Back in his cab, Jack takes a deep breath. He steals a quick, reluctant glance at the Corvette convertible next to him and the young lady driving it. The sun shines, but Jack is tired and when he closes his eyes he see the sparklers of a deep eye rub. He interprets the star-dots to be armies surrounding thin rivers. Jack wonders if he might be going a little nuts, needing a little break from the road. It has been years.

A half hour later Jack is back on the freeway and he notices the white Corvette along side of him, evenly, humming without effort. Jack wonders what her life must be like. Alone, on I-26, South Carolina. It is late June, hot and humid. Jack's air is on the fritz, has been for a long time. Why would anyone take a dose of the South, even a small one, this time of year, Jack asks himself.

Suddenly Jack's car phone whistles and this startles him. Besides, didn't the tiny batteries die several states ago? And he hasn't paid his service fee in years. Jack wonders if he's not confused, if it's not really the CB.

But the phone rings again.

Jack says "Hello" only to hear someone say, "Talk to strangers." That is it. "Talk to strangers." Nothing else, but a click on the other end.

Wrong number, Jack finally concludes. What are the odds. And in a moment he dismisses the transaction completely.

In the distance Jack sees a person, thumb in the air but off

83

to the side of her hip. The Corvette blows by; Jack's not even an afterthought.

He pulls over and waits until the hitchhiker catches up with his rig. And he waits. Jack looks into his rearview mirror and waits some more. Though the hiker has turned to Jack, that is all. No movement.

Jack hops out of his cab, approaches the hiker.

She is dressed in layers of white, and she has a jumble of wicker baskets at her feet. She is dark with purple bruises around her eyes and she looks sad and tired and lonely.

"Can I offer you help?" Jack asks.

Speechless, Jack views her life's pain in her eyes. She has a strangely anonymous way of climbing into his truck, deflecting attention from herself without making any great effort. Jack helps her into the cab. He loads all of the baskets into the trailer, except for one, which she insists on holding inside the cab. It is special, she tells him.

Eventually, about 20 miles later, Jack learns that her name is Janie. He learns that she is running away from home, and from a husband who beats her up. Regularly. She looks to be 50-something, though Jack could be way off. She confides in him that luckily she has no children, but she says it as though she can hardly see the luck in it at all.

She weaves baskets and sells them for money. Along the highway to Charleston.

"Beautiful," Jack remarks. This is his word for '*I understand your pain. Your baskets are wonderful and God loves you.*'

"My husband drives truck," she informs Jack, finally making eye contact. Concern creases a face that is serene, maybe angelic. "That's why I wasn't so sure I wanted a ride from another . . ."

"Truck driver." Jack finishes her sentence.

The price tag label sticks up from her homemade basket like a white tongue, lolling from the re-circulated air in his cab. Jack thinks it says "$10 or best offer."

She perspires.

"Sorry, but my air is on the blink."

She shrugs. Beads of sweat rest on her skin like raindrops on flower petals.

"I'm poor and I'm black and I have no skills and no kids and now no husband," she tells Jack. "I'm sitting in the cab of another trucker, only this truck doesn't have a name on it. No Kroger or Wal-Mart or anything. For all I know, you could be some crazed criminal. Some escaped felon. Right now, my life is kinda in your hands, Mister. So air conditioning's about the very last thing on my mind right this moment." She is again unable to make eye contact with Jack.

He manages a small smile.

She smiles too, finally, though Jack thinks she might be on the verge of tears.

"For you have been born again,
not of perishable seed, but of imperishable,
through the living and enduring word of God."
—*1 Peter 1:23*

She asks Jack where he's headed, and Jack asks in return if she has any friends. She tells him she has a sister who moved to Valdosta 20 years ago, and so Jack indicates that, ironically enough, Valdosta is where he's headed. But that he would need some directions getting there.

Again, she smiles.

Though this woman has her own set of problems, she seems quite interested in Jack's. She can't figure him out. That's okay, Jack thinks, but he doesn't wish for her to fear him. She's coming from an environment full of that.

"So, what is it again you deliver?" she asks.

"Nothing," Jack says.

"You're serious?"

"As a deacon."

Again, Jack catches her smiling. Her large brown eyes are set close together, giving her gaze an added intensity when she laughs.

"So you just wander the South in search of hitchhikers, and when you find one you become their personal escort."

"Not really," Jack confesses. "Actually, I was taught never to talk to strangers. And never, never pick up hitchhikers. I don't make it a habit. I would like to help them, but usually they need only a ride. Nothing else. You looked like you needed more, you know, with the baskets."

"Lord, do I. Need more, I mean."

"So this is what I do."

A dreadful look crosses her face. "I can't pay you, you know. Either money or the other. I don't do that."

"No problem," Jack assures her. "I just want to help you find a safe place."

"Okay," she says, her voice not completely free of curiosity. "Okay, now that we understand each other." She manages another weak smile. A small tear enters her eye. "Earl."

"Pardon me?"

"My husband. Earl. That's his name. I am deathly worried about him."

This throws Jack. Didn't she just explain to him that he hurts her quite often?

"He can't take care of himself. He's helpless as a baby."

The headlights of an American Van Lines truck wash over him. More people moving. Jack watches after he passes him, studies the size of the trailer, the truck and its contents plunging toward someone's new home, disappearing into the corpse of night.

Janie explains that her brother forced her to marry Earl, as he owed Earl a good deal of money. From an accumulation of small loans, debts from card games, and various favors over the years. Though it is the year 2001 and not 1945, freedom is still defined in many different ways. Janie had no other choices. Her brother would have made life very difficult for her had she not gone along with the plan. Her mother and father had both died young, plantation help in South Carolina. Now there was just Earl, as even her brother was no longer to be found. Rumor had it he moved to New Orleans.

Inside a Life

Today she lives in crude poverty among a bank of migrant worker huts. Earl drives a truck and sees her every other weekend.

He never gives her money for groceries or anything else. Thus, the baskets. Weaving was a skill her mother had taught her. The basket at her feet in the cab of Jack's truck was one actually made by her mother, given to Janie 30 years ago. Though the tag claims it goes for $10, she hasn't brought herself to sell it.

"Beautiful," Jack says, this time softly.

Fall in June

23.

*"God is not unjust; he will not forget your work and the love
you have shown him as you have helped his people
and continue to help them. "*
—Hebrews 6:10

Jack pulls his truck up to her sister's front door and helps
her out of the cab. Valdosta's heat cups him like a priest's collar, a
giant one, embracing his entire body. Unlike Janie, he is not used
to this oppression.

They are met at the front door by an elderly woman with
high cheekbones and the sad eyes of an ex-slave. She wears a red
rayon bathrobe and black Converse tennis shoes. They squeak on
the planked floor just as they might in Madison Square Garden.

Her name is Dorothia, and she shakes Jack's warm hand,
before hugging Janie for a good 40 seconds. When they release,
Jack notes the veins in their hands and arms are as hard and long as
electrical wires.

By the looks in their eyes, Jack realizes how close they are,
though they haven't seen each other in two decades. Nor spoken.

"Earl?" Dorothia asks.

"One too many times," Janie says darkly. Dorothia knows
what she means.

"Are you all right?"

"I'm just scared," Janie admits, tonelessly.

Dorothia's sallow cheeks make her appear as though she
hasn't had a meal in months. Like her sister, cordlike veins bulge
from her taut neck. Her lips are cracked and dry. The palms of her
hands are white as sugar and her legs are scrawny as licorice root.

Fall in June

Janie catches on.

"Somebody's dead," she says. The words sound like someone ripping pieces of flesh out of Janie's throat. Their faces are stonily unreadable to Jack.

"Janie . . ."

They are again face-to-face, Janie's chest heaving. A wheezing noise emerges from deep within. It is obvious to Jack that words fail Dorothia.

He turns slightly away.

They gather each other in a painful embrace.

"No, Sister, no," Janie wails. "Tell me not you. Tell me not you!" Her voice is quietly furious.

Jack stands in the doorway, his eyes fixed on his truck. He stares dumbly, realizing he has delivered Janie to be with her sister while she is dying. Cancer. But instead of fear and regret and anger in Dorothia's voice, Jack hears something else. He hears genuine joy, as she proclaims, "Jane, I am on my way to see Him. And I have never, never been happier in my entire 69 long years of life!"

"The man who does the will of God lives forever."
—1 John 2:17

Light seeps from beneath Dorothia's bedroom door as Jack quietly prepares to leave her small home. Janie sits on an old orange couch in the living room, sipping tea, the TV on mute, casting shadows in the tiny box. She gives him a small hug goodbye and offers to pay him some of the $60 she has left to her name. Of course Jack declines, and offers to pray for her and Dorothia. A part of him wants to say goodbye to her sister, but another part wishes to slip quietly into the thick Georgia humidity and continue on his way, back to Iowa.

"At least take this." Janie offers Jack the special wicker basket she held on her lap in his truck. "As I said, Momma made this one. It was her last."

"Beautiful," is all Jack can think to say.

"Thank you," Janie says. She smiles thinly. Her neck and temples glisten with sweat.

"Dorothia, your sister. She is so . . . so happy. And for good reason. She understands things."

Once on the road, Jack feels alone and lonely. And tired. After a few miles he begins to notice the billboards again:

"LIQUOR WAREHOUSE—3 MILES"
"ASIAN MASSAGE—NEXT EXIT"
*"SONYA'S GENTLEMEN'S CLUB—CLOSER THAN
YOU THINK"*

The Arranged Hour

There is truth to the saying that a man alone is much easier prey than one in the safety of someone's home. Like Dorothia's. Jack remembers the rusty saw under the seat, then realizes he is too tired.

Back on the highway to Iowa, Jack weeps for Janie and her sister, thanks God for Sid, out there somewhere, and longs to see Paula and her sons—one last time. He wonders if the courts are considering Ronnie's confession. Sparing Jay's life. Giving Paula hope. Jack is drawn back to them, time and again, just as he was once drawn to this truck in the first place.

Going Back to Another Life
25.

"Therefore do not worry about tomorrow,
for tomorrow will worry about itself."
—*Matthew 6:34*

Finally, the needle moves. Dances, twitching like a nervous trigger finger on an unsure gun.

Running out of gas, Jack is not surprised to see the *REST STOP ONE MILE* sign. God works this way. He smiles at His faithfulness. His love. His way of working things out for Jack, though he doesn't deserve them to work out.

It's hot, and Jack imagines what it's like to refuel, standing at the pumps, watching the numbers rise on the tank.

But now he has less than 1/16th of a tank of diesel left. And less than ten bucks in his pocket.

Jack notices how busy the rest stop is, wonders quickly if this is a holiday weekend. It's mid-August, so unless Hallmark added one, it is just a regular Wednesday.

In his cab, before turning the ignition toward him for the last time, he says a prayer. He reflects. He prays for Paula and for her sons Jay and Ronnie. That Paula finds more peace. That Jay and Ronnie are on an eternal stay of execution with the Lord. He prays for Floyd, the minister of all that God designed for him to do. His service above self. His love for service, that it may only grow from here—if that's even possible. He prays for Professor Max, that he never gets too smart to understand Jesus. To not only know about Him, but to know *Him*. He prays for Willie and his friends, that they may get it. Get it before it's too late.

Jack prays for the crippled man in northern Michigan, that

93

he may continue to visit the small white church, both when it is open and when it is not. That the Lord may quiet his anger, his bitterness. That He may one day heal him completely.

The millionaire, in Iowa. Until now, he's been able to buy anything he wants. *Everything* he wants. Now let him receive the gift he can't buy. Grace.

Jack prays for Tax Law, that He may look kindly on her. Despite all. That she may look for and truly find Him, and that she may ask Him for His forgiveness. And Jack prays for Janie and Dorothia and also for Earl. And he prays for gas.

Jack flips his ignition and the engine dies. He sits in his cab, the cool air vent waning, until his prayers are complete. He re-reads his fuel gauge for the tenth time. But this time the needle rises, gradually, to a quarter tank. And not on its own. Then there is a moment of consoling silence before Jack realizes he's forgotten someone. That man, from the prison. Who runs the diner in Arizona. Who runs away from the Truth, daily.

"Oh, Lord," Jack says, aloud. "May he be caught so that he may be freed."

"I am the vine; you are the branches.
If a man remains in me and I in him,
he will bear much fruit;
apart from me you can do nothing."
—John 15:5

The crimson paint is fresh and thick in the generic can Jack holds cupped in his right hand. There is an outdated Ryder truck in the spot next to him. The weary man in the driver's side watches. He looks oddly familiar to Jack. Before long, the man offers Jack a three-foot stepladder and he's in business.

The man scrutinizes this with extreme curiosity as Jack begins to paint. As he begins to form letters. Not with a brush, but with a large white t-shirt he was tired of wearing.

And Jack spells, on one side of his long, white trailer:

Jesus Trucking Company

Then on the other. In the brightest crimson red he's ever seen.

Finally, the fellow who offered Jack his ladder offers now to help him work. Help clean up the letters. Penmanship never was one of Jack's strengths. At first he is content just holding the ladder in place with his boot while Jack attempts on his own to straighten what is anything but neat. Then, impatiently, he asks if he can just borrow the shirt. Do it for Jack. Jack gladly hands it over.

"Wait a minute!" he declares, rummaging through the trailer of his Ryder. He finds a paintbrush. He is all smiles as he works on cleaning up the print. He works diligently, while Jack now holds the ladder for him.

The man tells Jack his name is George. Is anyone actually named George anymore, Jack wonders.

"Where are you moving?" he asks George.

"I'm not exactly moving," he answers. "It's more like *running*."

George volunteers his story. How first he became addicted to gambling. How five years ago his wife decided to end their marriage. How on one Father's Day he'd had the kids over to his apartment. This was during the separation period, when things *appeared* to be improving. How he'd had too much to drink and how he'd swerved into the other lane on his way to take his kids home to his wife. How his car had collided with an oncoming vehicle. How his daughter Tess had died a few hours later in ER.

Then George confessed how he'd just been released from doing time—convicted of gross negligence and vehicular manslaughter. How he blamed himself for so much, including ending the life of his only daughter, Tess.

"So, I'm not so much moving as I am running." He lights a cigar. Three plumes of smoke curl from his nose. "On the day of my release from prison, my father greeted me in the warden's lobby. Said he'd bought me this Rider truck. That's right, *bought* it. Said to me, 'Get out of here, George. You're a disgrace to us all.' So I'm 'getting.'"

Jack looks through his Bible, and he shows George the first verse that catches his eye: "*Yet to all who received him, to those who believed in his name, he gave the right to become children of God.*"

George puts his head down. Not so much in shame as in humble release.

"That's from John 1:12," Jack tells him.

"John who?" George asks. He holds his cigar between his forefinger and thumb, but doesn't smoke it.

Jack spends the next hour telling George not so much about John as about Jesus. But Jack eventually comes back to John. "Here, read this, George."

He does.

"Now aloud," Jack instructs him.

George pauses, then stares at Jack with suspicion. Perhaps he is recalling the lottery tickets, still trying to make sense of that. He then lets the cigar drop from his fingers to the asphalt.

"For God so loved the world that he gave his one and only son, that whoever believes in him shall not perish but have eternal life."

Jack smiles. "That's John 3:16," he says.

"John 3:16," George repeats. "I've seen it at football games. In the end zones. I always thought it was a joke of some kind."

"It's no joke, George. It's the one truth."

George thinks on it. "But this can't apply to me. I mean, look at the mess I made. Nothing or nobody can fix it."

"Yes, George, this applies even to you. *Especially* to you if you come to Jesus. And what's even greater is that He's already fixed things. He fixed them before they even broke. And you can rely on Him for guidance and strength and peace—even in light of the mess you've made. Today, tomorrow. And every day."

George cries.

"So you can face situations."

"So what you're saying is that he's, like, with you?"

"Yes."

"All the time?"

"All the time."

George places the toe of his right boot over the lit end of his cigar. Then he twists, as if snuffing out the life of a poisonous bug. When he adjusts his foot, the pavement resembles the forehead of a Catholic on Ash Wednesday.

"Even now?"

"Even now."

Digging for Hope
27.

*"For whoever wants to save his life will lose it,
but whoever loses his life for me will find it."*
—Matthew 16:25

When George finishes touching up Jack's paint job, he begins on his own trailer. His is a full pull with mud-flaps featuring silhouetted ladies propped back on the palms of their hands. It takes George several coats of white paint, also found in his hauler, to cover all of the yellow and black, trademark colors of Ryder.

People at the rest stop stare at George. He works for hours. By sunset, a police officer pulls up beside the Ryder, questions George. Questions Jack.

"Is it against the law to paint here?" George asks the officer.

"Quite honestly, I can't tell you." He goes by Officer Jennings and he is tall and has a thin, though kind face. Jack thinks he's new on the job because he begins to read them their rights from a 3 by 5 card.

"If it is, no problem," Jack interrupts officer Jennings. Creating a scene is the last thing on Jack's mind.

"Normally people just stop here and . . . rest," he explains, moving his hands in the air to describe things, his face changing to confusion. "Not to paint their vehicles."

"We understand," George tells him. "Completely."

"We will stop if you'd like, Officer," Jack says.

A crowd has gathered. Some parents instruct their children to run to the car and lock the doors. One man stands, his mouth wide open, as if he's fallen upon free, though interesting, entertainment.

99

Digging for Hope

"Let me just ask you," Officer Jennings says, his head tilted as if listening for termites in a doorframe. He slips the 3 by 5 card into his shirt pocket. "So, what's this all about?"

Jack doesn't know where to begin.

So George begins for him. "It's easy, Sir. We just met. I have been lost my entire life. If you run a felony check on me, you'll find that I've done some time. Nothing pre-meditated, just poor, poor choices. I am still lost. But I'm in my forties and until the last few hours I haven't had a clue where to go next. Nor how to get there. So I'm pulled over here, just stopped like all the rest of the folks around here. Almost ready to get back on the road. The road to nowhere. And suddenly I see this man, this guy here." George nods to Jack. Jack smiles and shrugs.

"And he's painting these words on his truck. And I approach him just like you did me. And I ask him what he's doing, just like you did me. And when I find out, I decide to offer him some help. Offer him my little stepladder. And then I start helping him. And it wasn't a decision *I made* as much as it was a decision *made for me*. Hard to understand, I know. Hard to explain, too."

Officer Jennings now notices the audience. About 60 people have gathered. They want to see what he will say, what he'll order Jack and George to do. A few must be hoping, though privately, for a ticket to be issued. Perhaps for a brawl to break out.

"In between painting his truck and mine," George adds, "he told me about Jesus. Enough that I want to learn more. So this brings you up to date."

Officer Jennings checks his watch. He grows a little impatient. He knows the crowd waits for him to rule. Finally he says, more out of thoughtfulness than anger, "Guys, why don't you try to wrap this up in, say, half an hour or so."

George grins, as if he's eaten the pie off a windowsill. "That can be done, Sir."

Officer Jennings slips into his squad car, makes some notes on a notepad, and drives off. The crowd dissolves like slow-motion fireworks. A few onlookers appear disappointed. Others offer to help George finish his paint job. A young boy presses his face into the window of a Ford Taurus, and his nose and mouth flatten like rotting peaches. His eyes are fixed on the departing police cruiser. Then an elderly lady and a very young girl approach Jack. They could be great grandmother and great granddaughter, their ages are so far apart.

Great grandmother asks Jack if he'd care to talk a moment. Her tone is unsure and she looks vaguely at his eyes. Her chest heaves and Jack sees that she's been crying.

"Tell us," she asks. "Tell us what you told him. Please." She points, accusingly, to George. "Please."

> *"Carry each other's burdens and in this way you will fulfill the
> law of Christ."*
> —*Galatians 6:2*

George follows Jack in the event he runs out of gas on his
way back to the Iowa State Penitentiary. The needle on Jack's gas
gauge reaches less than 1/32nd of a tank, though it hasn't budged
for three states. Jack marvels at this, yet another miracle He per-
forms.

On the way, Jack stops at Paula's restaurant to check on her,
get a report. See how she's doing. But there is only one car out
front. Inside is the owner, Jack presumes, sitting at the counter, a
highball glass full of orange juice resting on a paper place mat. His
stomach burst through his shirt with rock hard obesity. A stubbed
cigar smolders in a nearby ashtray.

"Where is everyone?" Jack asks, trying to avoid the dead
air.

"Everyone?" he asks back. He rolls the glass in his palms.
"Could you get more specific?"

"Paula."

His eyes flex in surprise that Jack doesn't know. Dandruff
spots his eyebrows and lashes.

"Ronnie," he says, flatly. His mouth forms an unintention-
al smile, though it's one of pain, not joy. Not in the least. He wears
a three-day shadow on his tired, large face. "I used to coach him in
little league baseball. He was absolutely no good. No good at all.
Everyone teased him. I'd stick him in right field with two outs in
the last inning. It could be that it's my fault he turned out the way

he did. That *I* am responsible. Today, a kid needs hope. To believe in something. It's called self-esteem. You read all kinds of things about that today. What did we know about it then?" He buries his face in his arms and cries uncontrollably.

"Today?" Jack states, referring to Ronnie's date with death. Jack feels his voice catch in his throat. George stands in the empty parking lot, kicking stones like a nine-year-old boy waiting for his father.

"Last night," the owner clarifies. "11:44 p.m., to be exact. I think the whole town's stayin' away from here, either in honor of Paula, or maybe for fear of running into her." His voice now sounds a little querulous as he explains to no one in particular. "I'm sorry, Paula. I'm sorry I never let the kid play anything but right field. I was just afraid he'd mess up is all. Cost us the game. Drop a ball. Or throw it to the wrong base. What's it matter now, though."

Jack wants to ask him this next question, but he's a bit fearful of the answer. He somehow develops the courage. "Jay?" Jack's eyes travel down to the diner floor in anticipation of his response.

"Jay's okay," he says, windswept. "Was released two days ago. Apparently Ronnie fessed up. And Jay let him, which surprised everyone, as close as they were."

Jack breathes a slight sigh of relief, but gives great thanks.

"Watched his brother die," he adds. "Watched him. Story is Jay screamed so loud it was like he was the one being punished. Which maybe he was." He lowers his head one last time. "Jay. I put him at shortstop. Starting shortstop. He never missed a game, never missed an inning. Lead the league in putouts. He always found a way to make the out." Finally, his son emerges from the kitchen. He pours his pop some fresh coffee, and then offers Jack a cup. He refuses, politely.

Outside the place called EAT, Jack looks for George, fills him in. Jack finds George replacing his mud flaps with a long Craftsman screwdriver. They are now two symbols of fish. Wordlessly they decide to find Paula. And Jay. Their motors start, one after the other, sudden and piercing, like two old coughing men, hacking lungs sounding soggy as wet sponges.

Choosing to Believe
29.

"Be kind and compassionate to one another."
—Ephesians 4:32

The lights are on above the Laundromat where Paula lives. Below, clusters of news reporters camp, waiting for her or Jay to come down. An interview here will help their station's ratings, propel their careers upward.

Public Works has arranged fluorescent red sawhorses around the building. Jack stretches over one, ducks under another.

Once upstairs, Jack is concerned he may have no words inside him for Paula or for Jay. But before he knows it, a brief prayer comes to mind, asking God for wisdom and compassion. George stays outside, stands near his truck.

No one answers Paula's door, so Jack slowly, gently enters her room. Inside, the buttery light is soft, like margarine melting together with skim milk. Her apartment smells like a wet dog. The walls are mortared in odd patches, some of them vaguely resembling stick figures. She owns one couch, its floral pattern curling in worn, ashy petals. A souvenir in the form of an anorexic sea gull sits on top of a wooden crate that once transported Florida oranges. The time on a tiny Sony clock radio surges on and off in split-second unison, evident of a brief power outage. The unnerving thought of the town losing electricity at the exact moment of Ronnie's electrocution triggers an icy flash up Jack's spine, then worms off in other directions of his body, causing him to feel faint.

Jack then hears something, weeping he thinks, coming from a small alcove off to the side. It is Paula.

Without word, Jack enters her bedroom, sits beside her on

the floor. She tries to manage her pain, but it is intense, an invisible geography whose terrain shifts invasively by the second. Jack embraces her gently and searches deeply inside his heart for the right words—words that might help. Her eyes are cracked networks of red veins.

Jack realizes here that it is not difficult to be like Jesus, it is impossible.

The two hold each other, again without words, for hours of uncontrolled grief. Finally, Jack's curiosity too strong to resist, he asks about Jay's whereabouts.

"His father," she answers. "He's with his father."

"What has happened to me really served to advance the gospel."
—Philippians 1:12

Jay and Ronnie had not seen their father for over 20 years. He deserted the three of them when both boys were young, under five. He never saw Jay play shortstop and never saw Ronnie ride the bench. But less than one hour before Ronnie's execution, he appeared at the warden's office with a plea to be reunited with his sons.

Over coffee, Paula tells Jack and George that his name is Lyman and that today he drives truck. This next part warms Jack's heart. "He's different now. Much different."

"How so?" George asks. Jack somehow knows what's coming next. After all, wherever he was, whatever he was doing, he made it to say goodbye to his son Ronnie.

"He's just not the same person who abandoned us 22 years ago," Paula explains. "He's a Christian. We're all four of us in this small conference room, before they were to, you know. We was alone and together for what's the first time in over two decades and for the last time ever. And he says he's sorry. Sorry for leaving us. Sorry for everything. He explains how things would have had a different outcome had he hung around 20 years ago. How he'd have been here for the boys. And for me. That he's made some big mistakes, and maybe those mistakes are what really lead to Ronnie's situation."

Paula jabs at her red eyes with powder blue Kleenex.

"But that recently, very recently, he's become saved. He uses that word. And he says it like it's got three syllables. *Sa-ve-*

ed. Said he's been reading about this case in the USA Today and that he's prayed with all his broken heart what to do. His heart finally told him that he had to come here to be with Ronnie. And Jay. And me."

George sits on the edge of Paula's flower couch. His eyes are red too.

"Where are they now?" Jack asks.

Paula laughs, briefly, through her tears. "They're out . . . driving. Driving around, I guess."

"Driving around?"

"Yes," she adds. "Lyman's learning his son a trade. Trucking. He's got this big, long trailer. A full pull, he calls it. I think the front is in a different zip code than the back, it's so long. And he's learning Jay how it all works."

Jack can see from his expression that George is dying to ask the question.

"Go ahead, George," Jack encourages him. "Ask her."

George peers deeply into Paula's wounded eyes. He inches forward on her old ratty couch. And he asks. "If you don't mind me asking, Paula. Who does Lyman drive truck for?"

Paula sighs, then shrugs. "You mean what company?"

"Exactly."

"I never asked," she said. "All's I know is there's these big initials on both sides of his pull that says **J T C**. Whatever that is."

Jack's eyes meet George's. They smile. George cries until he is speechless, circling his fingertips over his cheekbones where little eggs rise. Finally he manages, in between sobs, to ask her one more question. "Paula, would those initials be in red?"

"Yes, they are," she answers. "As a matter of fact they are."

Collecting
31.

*"Fathers, do not exasperate your children; instead, bring them up
in the training and instruction of the Lord."*
—*Ephesians 6:4*

The place called EAT is full again. It has been only a week
since Ronnie's death, but Paula is back to work. Jack is surprised
to see the change of atmosphere in the old, dreary truck stop diner.
Customers are cheerful and friendly. Talkative. The owner has
shaved, and today wears a happy face. Even Paula's attitude seems
brighter.

Around a large round table, Lyman explains grace, of all
things, as George and his son Jay listen intently. George has his
eyes fixed on Lyman, a smile worming over his face. At the counter Jack notices a man wearing a K-Mart cap eavesdropping on the
discussion. His eyes are wide and shiny.

"We see Satan all over the world," Lyman says at one point.
"Everywhere you look almost. There's greed, there's dishonesty,
there's lust. Lots of that going around. There's things so bad that
only man could have invented them. Trouble is in those places, let
me tell you. But peace is found only in Jesus."

Lyman is not loud or gregarious or even self-righteous.
Instead he explains with humility, with a sense of purpose.

"In the end, living for Him is all that matters most. I just
wanted Ronnie to have God as his destination. And it appears as
though he did. Ask Jay." Here, Lyman speaks specifically to
George.

"You bet," Jay says, somewhat sheepishly. "His last words
were '*No one comes to Him except through Jesus.*' Something like
that."

Collecting

Jack watches as the man in the K-Mart cap ignores his scrambled eggs. Hash browns sit on the large plate like a pile of thin white worms. His face shows a strange disturbance.

"Tell him," Lyman says. "Tell him Jay what it was like, Ronnie's last few days."

Jay sips at his coffee but doesn't get any. His eyes tighten and expand in intelligent perusal. "Well, he was always reading the Bible lately. It was like once he got his hands on it, he couldn't let go. And it's all he wanted to talk about. Sure he was sorry for what he'd done, but he told me he'd been forgiven. That he was ready to accept responsibility. And that he didn't need any more stays of execution. He'd been gifted enough. That was the word he used— 'gifted'." Across his face is a convincing, placid wisdom.

Lyman places a large, red arm around his son's frail shoulder. A good two minutes elapse without words.

"Peace," Jay adds at last. "Ronnie was at such peace with himself at the end."

The man at the counter removes his cap, stands, and wanders over to the round table. His face is sizzling red, like the interior of a 1960 Corvair. Shyly he asks, "Mind if I join you a bit?"

Lyman spends his nights at the only motel in town, the Sail-Inn. The world is so full of irony. There is no water within a 300-mile radius of this tiny town, yet someone named this place the Sail-Inn.

There he keeps his truck at night while teaching his youngest son Jay to drive it during the day. Lyman also spends some time helping the man who used to work for K-Mart repaint the side of his truck. Yes, Jay still harbors bitterness and resentment about his father deserting him, but Jay also understands forgiveness now. Soon, Jay will be ready to get licensed. Once that occurs, Jack has no doubt that, considering the influence of his teacher, Jay too will be driving for Jesus.

Settling into the Earth

32.

"Therefore, if anyone is in Christ, he is a new creation;
the old has gone, the new has come!"
—*2 Corinthians 5:17*

Saying goodbye to them is not an easy thing. Especially to Paula and George. But it is necessary, as something Jack can't quite explain draws him back to the southwestern states. He believes he'll have enough gas to get there. Having more faith than actual fuel helps.

Just before Jack's rig breaks down, he notices, for the first time, the number of mini-storage units popping up everywhere, from Iowa to Arizona. They seem to be reproducing on their own.

Our obsession with MORE, he concludes. It is just before his engine dies that he comes up with a list of things that were not around when he was in college: espresso coffee, the World Wide Web, caller ID. Sports utility vehicles, also known as SUVs. Considering he's broken down, one of those right now might be nice.

All these nice things, yet today he sees more depression in people than ever. Or maybe Jack just notices it more. More fragile relationships. More children giving birth to children. More self-storage buildings to keep the things we can no longer live without, but can't keep at our homes. So much of our time and money and energy are spent on areas of our life—areas other than God. And yet it is He who gives us all things.

Including the SUV that pulls up to him; the driver, too, who leans out his window and offers Jack a ride into town.

His name is Juan and he is a minister. On the drive to town, Juan tells Jack his story. Originally from Mexico, he was raised in a badly broken family of 16 children. He tells Jack that he, like all his brothers and sisters, dropped out of school at an early age. All got into trouble, and each of his brothers has done some time in jail. Three of his four sisters are either drug addicts or prostitutes or both.

Juan's other sister, Maria, had three children of her own by the time she was 21 years old.

Remarkably, Juan somehow turned his life around. At age 23, he returned to school, and then continued on to seminary. Today, he travels from one Hispanic community to another and preaches the Word of the Lord. He spends a great deal of his time counseling at-risk families along the way.

"How?" Jack asks Juan. "How were you able to change? To break the cycle?"

Juan thinks about it briefly. "Many people believe that failure is a curse," he says. "That the patterns established are too strong to break. For me, it was a matter of digging up my past, you know, sort of downloading the truth into my life, asking God for the strength to deal with it once and for all and then forget about it, and finally going directly to God with my prayer to change."

Juan takes his eyes off the road for this next part, and looks Jack squarely in the eye. "As Paul said, '*But one thing I do: Forgetting what is behind and straining toward what is ahead.*' My life's motto."

In town, Juan purchases the parts he believes he needs to get Jack back on the road again. Back at the truck, he removes the injector with surgeon-like skill. With the dangling wires and viscid black grease, Juan looks like he's severed an animal's head. He attaches the new, slightly oversized injector, fastens it tightly, and Jack's back in business. Quickly, Juan apologizes for having to run. He's worried about a man who is meeting his father for the first time in over 40 years. The father is old and crippled and is being escorted down here from Iowa by a team of legal eagles. Oh, and he is worth over 30 million dollars. He fathered the son, Lupe, during a brief affair years ago with a migrant worker named Isabel. Afterward, he relocated to some small, anonymous town in Iowa in order to be anonymous himself. Juan hopes to counsel them all and help them to the Lord.

As Juan drives away, Jack thanks him and the Lord for SUVs. Especially for white ones driven by Hispanic ministers who paint **JESUS TRUCKING CO.** on both doors in, of course, red.

Climbing Back, Climbing Out
33.

"And the Lord added to their number daily those who were being saved."
—Acts 2:47

Paused along the California coast, a trip Jack's always wanted to take, he watches sailboats lift and drop in the swelling sea. Though the sky is the color of bad teeth, the overall view of the ocean, the sand, the mountains, is unrivaled. The silhouette of a man on a Sunfish parallels the plane of the ocean. From where Jack sits it appears the man wears no life jacket.

Jack steps down from his cab, strolls the beach, and combs it for sand dollars. He's never found one unbroken. The sound of the sea sudsing the rocks has a violent effect to it. Jack is surprised to come across a teenager, alone, sitting, perched totemically in the sand. Her skin is the color of Irish cream, and she wears dangly silver earrings. Each earring is a dancing Indian. Her dark black hair is pulled back from her forehead and bound to form a ponytail long as an African snake. She is thin as smoke, sunburned, shoeless, dreamlike.

Jack respects her privacy until he notices the empty bottle of pills sitting upside-down in the sand.

"Are you okay, Miss?" Jack asks, moving closer, tentative in his approach. He momentarily wonders if she's been hypnotized by the sea.

She wears sleek Oakley sunglasses, hugging her dark face, and a T-shirt that says: *"I'm not indecisive . . . am I?"*

"I just want something simple," she answers, to no one in particular. She wears a haunted look, her eyes nearly crystalline.

Climbing Back, Climbing Out

"Excuse me?" Jack approaches her, scooping up the empty bottle with his hand. The label reads Extra-Strength Tylenol. She doesn't move. Jack gently touches her thin shoulder, shakes her as softly as possible. She gasps, her shiny eyes popping open, looking straight ahead, as if studying the ocean for secrets.

"The simple life," she continues, trancelike. "Quitting school. Work. Move to a farm. Do just enough to stay alive. Eat Spam for lunch. Maybe something a little more complicated for dinner, but not much!" Her breath smells vaguely like strawberry Bubblicious Bubble Gum.

Next to her on the sand is the copy of a popular teen magazine. Granules of sand cover the model's face.

"You're not in a very good place," Jack tells her, wanting to help. He says a silent prayer that his voice would sail through the floodplain of acetaminophen to some small island of sobriety within her.

"I woke up this morning in a Los Angeles gutter," she says. "Wanting to be alone but not by myself. I could see everything so clearly, but I had no control over anything. Over what happened. Somehow I managed to hitchhike here. Wherever here is."

Her name, she volunteers, is Randi Smallbone, a Native American—lost in her own country. She slowly scissors her legs in the sand as if making a snow angel from the waist down. Propped only by her arms, Jack notices a scar, a perfect reddish pink circle centered in the hallow recesses of her left wrist.

"My family has fallen apart. Completely apart. Alcohol and drugs and eventually suicide. What's left of my reservation are pregnant women and sickly children. No one works. No one either lives or dies heroically anymore. How can evil have so much power? My people attract damage and dysfunction." She covers her mouth with a quivering hand.

Jack is able to convince Randi to get into his truck. He rushes her to the nearest Medi-Center. There they pump Randi's stomach. Jack watches the half-dissolved tablets filter upward through a thin white tube, fighting gravity all the way. It reminds him of the last beads of a thick vanilla milk shake firing up a twisted, transparent straw. He watches Randi cry squeezed, frugal tears as she realizes what she's done. Her breathing is very fast, short little sips that hardly lift her chest.

After four hours of recovery, Jack asks the doctor to examine her, give her a complete physical. She says Randi's fine, other than ankles so swelled they look like melons. Must be all the walking she's done. The doctor winks subtly at Jack in reference to the scar on her wrist.

Outside Jack offers to buy Randi a meal, help her on her way. He'd like to discuss her future even though she tells him she's used up all of hers. She declines, but instead reaches into her backpack and offers Jack a gift. It is a small clay statue of a seated Native American woman with nine Indian babies crawling all over her. Jack graciously accepts.

"What's missing from this?" Randi asks, a grim tightness in her jaw. She wears a complicated empty expression.

Jack knows but doesn't want to say.

"The father, of course. All our lives are filled with fathers we can hardly remember, and yet can never forget."

A large tear drops from Randi's left eye. "I was born on a highway. Literally, on some highway in South Dakota. My mother was driving alone, on her way to find work in Michigan. She carried nothing in this old white truck but clothes, some bread, and me. Some people helped her with me, and then afterwards she drove off, as if my life was simply a comma in her life's sentence. When I was old enough, she told me she became Christian after that night. Navajo Christian. And we were doing fairly okay as mother and daughter until she died of polio. All my life I remember her walking like she was a glass full of water that didn't wish to spill. She was only 34 years of age when she spilled."

After this, Jack convinces Randi to have breakfast with him. He is able to find a small nameless restaurant with a 21-inch Rainbow Trout mounted over the pink neon "OPEN" sign. There is no other identification. Inside, a single fly buzzes against a lampshade on the table.

"My mother was a model of hope and faith for my generation. She helped 'On Eagles' Wings,' forming 'Youthquakes,' events for young Native American Indian Christians. She taught us God's prescription for recovery in Acts 3:19, '*Repent, then, and turn to God, so that your sins may be wiped out, that times of refreshing may come from the Lord.*' This was so useful for us because, as young as we were, we were addicted to booze. Boys and girls alike. I learned that it was not a curse that was holding back God's blessing, but it was sin. You know, the liquor."

Randi's dark eyes dart around like a deer watching for a silent predator. Suddenly, her face breaks into tears.

"So when she died, everyone just picked up where we left off. Drinking and sinning as if everything my mother said was some TV commercial for a product no one wanted to buy. After she left, we just sort of lost hope in this world. *I* lost hope." Jack hands her the last napkin from a green plastic claw. "And here I am."

Randi reluctantly orders three eggs, sunny-side up, a tall stack of pancakes, bacon, whole-wheat toast, and two chocolate milks. Jack realizes that despite the years of hardship she's seen, she's still just a kid.

"Food's about all I still love in this world," she says. She then places her small hand over her mouth, forming a cup. By her eyes, Jack knows she's hiding a smile.

"Randi," Jack says to her. "I'd like you to consider living in God's world, not this one. In the world your mother lived in, after she had you."

"She didn't seem happy to me."

"Did she seem at peace?"

Randi studies the question. "Yes. Yes, I think she was at peace. Despite her legs."

"Randi, in God's world, weak legs don't exist. There's no alcohol or drugs or suicide or even gambling. There's no pain or loneliness. In God's world, anything comes from nothing. Sand runs up the hourglass. Life begins at death. Darkness becomes light."

"How?" she asks, just as her order arrives. "How do you live in God's world?"

"Through Jesus," Jack says. "First you get to know Jesus. And you start loving Him and you never stop loving Him."

"It's impossible for someone with my background to change," Randi counters. "There's too much bad. If there's a God, I broke his heart to pieces. There's no more Sacred Circle."

Suddenly Randi doesn't feel like eating.

"I got so desperate for help I tried pop psychology. I typed in 'self-help' on the Internet and over 150,000 sites and book titles came up. From *101 Ways to Transform Your Life* to *1001 Ways to Be Happy.* I even read a few. Nothings works. Nor did the piles of New Year's Resolutions I made."

Jack takes hold of Randi's hand. "It's because there's only

Climbing Back, Climbing Out

Climbing Back, Climbing Out

one way to change, Randi. One way only. Through God's power. Those books. Those 150,000 titles. The problem with them is humans wrote them all. They're from people who feel just like you. Humans won't do, Randi. Not where the heart's involved."

"All I want is . . . love. Perfect love. That's all."

"Randi." Jack pauses, briefly, for effect. "Only God's love is perfect. And by the way, you can't break His heart. It's impossible."

They leave the restaurant called "Open," hopeful that Randi heard at least part of what he had to tell her. It is a beautiful morning, warm and clear, the sky a perfect, vaporous blue. Before Jack and Randi part ways, he offers her $20. It is exactly half of what Jack has left to his name. Randi accepts it, not knowing that fact, for sure.

"I mean," Randi elaborates, clutching the twenty. "I've had love. Every kind you can think of. Borrowed love, dutiful love, love that hates, lost love, secret love, first love, last love, and all the loves in between. Love on the run, fickle love, hopeful love, dangerous love, blind love, consuming and obsessive love, and conditional love. Careless love, I've had that. Crazy love. Hopeless love. I've looked for love in all the wrong places, as the song says. I've had lovesick love, unrequited love, and jealous love. And I can't forget lost in love, trapped love, dysfunctional love, and even warped and demented love. I don't think there's any form of love left out there that I haven't tried. Except His love, whatever that looks like."

"And that can only be found in one place, Randi."

"Yea, right," she says, lacy red blood vessels in her crying eyes. "I've heard that one before."

Jack hands her his Holy Bible.

"What . . . what is this . . ."

"Heaven and earth will pass away, Jesus said, but my words will never pass."

In a moment she forms a slight smile of hope, her eyes sparkling with the determination of someone who chooses to live, and her haunted look unravels, washes away for good.

"For I am already being poured out like a drink offering . . .
I have finished the race, I have kept the faith."
—*2 Timothy 4:6-7*

Jack is in a small town, his last rest stop before his journey really begins.

Here, people hang their laundry on clotheslines where they flap, fall like parachutes when the breeze picks up. Jack was driving through when his truck didn't run out of gas, but he did. Fatigue, perhaps a small stroke, says the physician of the Heart Nursing Home. The highways of every state he traveled through spin toward him like cast nets, along with momentary blackouts, the world's film periodically skipping frames.

Jack lay in bed, Room 216, along with all of the possessions he owns—a beautiful wicker basket that sits on a small nightstand near the phone, and, next to it, a tiny clay statue of an Indian mother and her babies.

Jack's roommate is named Robert. He has fossil-colored, ropy hair and appears to be worse off than Jack. There are tubes coming and going in every direction. If he didn't know better, Jack would think his roommate was hooked up to travel to the moon. The largest oxygen mask Jack has ever seen covers half of Robert's old face. Out of the corner of Jack's left eye he sees a ventilator.

Robert can't talk, but neither can Jack. Strokes took that from both men. Jack's not sure if Robert had only a stroke, or if he has something else besides. His family discusses things, but Jack only half-follows the lines of conversation, the sound of blood coursing through Jack's old, diminishing body competing with all other noise.

Jack's skin is gray, his mouth is full of ulcers, his lips are cracked and bleeding. There's a small, though constant, ringing in his ears. Jack can't begin to connect the dots. But he is alive and he understands that neither he nor Robert is being kept that way by the wondrous advances of medical technology, but by the will of God.

Jack hasn't talked with anyone he knows in weeks, since he got off the phone with Jay. Jay's story is an amazing one. He has begun his own ministry, and he travels the country in a white van and speaks to people about God. Mostly in church youth groups and at summer Bible camps. Of course, both sides of Jay's van read **Jesus Trucking Co.** His father, Lyman, rides separately, in his own truck, and usually works with parents of broken families. They are very committed and quite successful in their ministry. What they mean by this is that they give all the glory of their work to Him.

"The great thing about our journey of faith is that we're going somewhere," Jay told Jack the last time they spoke on the phone. "We are looking forward to Christ's return, His ultimate victory, and His new creation. That hope should make a difference in how we live today, motivating us to be holy and blameless before God."

Eight years ago Jay didn't know who Christ is. Now he lives his life for Him.

It both amazes Jack and doesn't. It does because it is still hard to believe that he was able to witness effectively. And it doesn't because with Him, everything is possible.

Like what happens now.

Into Jack's room is a new aid. She has silver hair and large brown eyes, and carries a cloth diaper thrown over one shoulder.

Jack knows he knows her from somewhere, but he can't immediately place her. He thinks he might be having a real *senior moment*. If Jack could talk, he'd ask.

Her eyes, however, have troubles meeting Jack's at first, ricocheting off to her shoulder with the diaper. He stares at her as she scrawls something on a metal clipboard, and then hangs it near the door. She reaches nervously for the five-pound *Gray's Anatomy*, as if she needs to hold something to contain her nervousness.

She fixes Jack's pillow, checks the nutritional drip which feeds him. She remarks what a beautiful wicker basket. Finally, she holds his hand and tears begin to visit her beautiful eyes. Jack would give anything to be able to speak, to ask her what is up. Who she is. But that can't happen right now. Several months ago, perhaps. But not now.

"I know you remember me," she begins. Her soft voice sounds vaguely familiar, jars Jack's imperfect memory. And she says this with such confidence.

Jack grips the cool metal of the safety rail and stares over to her.

"Years ago. Many years ago, you and I used to work together. At the accounting firm. You specialized in investments. Me, in tax law." She pauses. Her eyes flicker from emotion. Jack realizes now who she is. "I got you fired. I ruined your life. And I am so very sorry."

At first, Jack thinks this is a small world. Too small. Or else he wonders if he is hallucinating, the effect of some of the new medication they're experimenting with. He then wonders for a moment what people dream about when they're in comas. Maybe stuff like this. But her face and voice become clearer to him by the minute.

Tax law sits on the corner of Jack's bed. She holds his hand. She weeps.

There is something about her eyes which tell him that he is not unconscious at all, but growing more lucid by the moment.

"I have tried to find you the past few years. To tell you. To apologize. You see, my life changed dramatically. After you got fired, things went well at first. I became partner and made lots and lots of money. More than I ever thought possible. I was a complete slave to greed. My self-esteem was high. Extremely high. After all, that's what all the pop-psychology books pitch—high self-esteem is all that counts. I worked the usual 60-hour week. I had cars and houses and vacation time-shares and just about everything that's important. But by age 45, I also had three failed marriages. No one was good enough for me. I felt so empty, it hurt to wake in the morning.

"Then, the bottom dropped out. The money I was earning and the things that I had weren't enough. I needed more. So I started 'finding' a little more here, a little more there. After six months I got caught. Embezzling. I thought I was getting away with it. Little did I know the other partners had checks in place to catch this sort of thing. The firm got very aggressive with me, mainly because they felt betrayed. Also, my third marriage was to the chief partner's son. It was strategic at the time."

Tax Law reaches for a Kleenex on Jack's nightstand. He just watches, wanting to tell her something. Anything. But words are worlds away from him.

"So I lost it all. I mean everything. With the penalties, in fact, I am still repaying my debt. After doing some time in a low security jail . . . okay, *prison*, I decided to go into nursing. You know, to try to turn my life around. Help someone for a change. I got this idea when I was at this church. Now this part is confusing to me, but maybe you'll understand it more than me. I had never been in a church before in my life except for weddings and funerals and twice on Christmas when I was young. Maybe once on Easter, I forget. But I had heard this one small church offered meals to people who are, let's say, in between things. Like me. Well, I was too proud to go to the Salvation Army or a soup kitchen.

"This church sounded like a good option to me. It was so pretty and small and there were all these teens running around, playing a game in the parking lot. Teens, with their whole lives before them. So I had lunch there, in the basement, and this guy comes up to me. I'm sitting alone, my head down, like I'm ashamed, which I was, and this guy comes up and introduces himself to me. He says his name is Jay. Jay something. Last name begins with a 'C', I think. So this Jay says he's working with the teens, switching them on to God, and he saw me come in and what does he do? He brings me to Christ.

"What never would have made any sense to me before made perfect sense to me now. For instance, everyone prescribes high self-esteem as the solution to low self-esteem, when in fact Romans 12:3 says we basically think too highly of ourselves to begin with and this is part of the problem. We need only to think highly of *Him*. Jesus. Once this became clear to me, I was on the way. But not *my* way, *His* way. '*He who loses his life for My sake will find it*,' it says in Matthew 10:39. This was a few years back, but I've come to know Jesus more every day since. And even though no nurse training school would have me, due to the criminal checks they do on candidates, I can live with myself.

"I finally found a place that helps you become an aid. In a facility like this. Actually, if you want the full story, this Jay helped me find the training and this job. What a warrior for God that man is. My goal too."

She places a cool washcloth on Jack's forehead. He feels his scalp tighten, the roots of his white hair aching where aged follicles contract.

"I just absolutely love this job. I love to help people in the little way that I can. I make minimum wage, the least I have earned since I was babysitting in middle school, but it doesn't matter. I'd do this the rest of my life if it's God's plan. Maybe travel the country and help those who can't help themselves in all fifty states. Dreams."

It's like a reality check hits Tax Law. She smiles as if knowing that is a far-fetched goal.

"Anyway . . . I live in subsidized housing about 3 miles away. I walk to work, but on lousy days I get a ride with Rita. Rita is the floor supervisor. You've no doubt heard her if you haven't seen her."

She stands and straightens her white outfit. She cries and again tells Jack she is sorry and that she hopes he will some day, in his heart, find forgiveness. Jack signals for a pad of paper and a pen. She accommodates. He writes, "I already have. Years and years ago."

Tax Law offers him a warm and long hug.

Jack reaches into the nightstand drawer and fingers the keys to his truck. Tax Law wants to help, but isn't sure what Jack is trying to accomplish. Finally, he grabs them. He holds them out to her. Her eyes widen. Then she takes them, humbly, and Jack points out the window toward the parking lot. To the truck. The one that says "**Jesus Trucking Company**" on the side, spelled in bright crimson letters.

"For you," Jack manages to say, the first words he's spoken in weeks.

"But . . ." she says, "I can't drive a truck. I've never driven a truck in my life."

Jack smiles at her. "Neither had I."

Similar to God waiting until Pentecost to give the Holy Spirit, Jack wonders if the miracle is in his speaking or in Tax Law's hearing. Jack offers her a tight smile, his cold lips blue like the silvery skin on ripe, Michigan plums.

Just before he dozes off, Jack's attention is drawn to his room's window view where a long, black station wagon backs up toward the building. A closer look and Jack finds that this is not a station wagon at all, but a large hearse. A long, flat black one. It fills his entire window like a painting in which the artist didn't allow for enough canvas overlap.

The driver hops out, as does the passenger. Both are tall men wearing dark suits with red ties. After a few minutes they return to Jack's view and load a long gurney through the back of the wagon. The driver looks terribly familiar to Jack. The name "Bob" comes to mind.

They drive off.

An elderly woman watches all this from the courtyard, and waves goodbye to her friend in the hearse as it were the end of a parade. She shuffles back to her room with the aid of a walker, not lifting her feet, her gown swallowing her up from the lawn. Once she is close enough Jack sees she is smiling, taking in the fickle spring sunshine.

All of this joy tires Jack out, especially the words painted in

white across the jet-black side panel of the hearse—
"**JESUS TRUCKING CO.**"—and cause Jack to sleep for a dozen dream-filled hours.

Driving Home

35.

"He appointed twelve—designating them apostles—that they might be with him and that he might send them out to preach . . ."
—Mark 3:14

She thanks Jack and offers him one last handshake, which eventually turns into a clumsy hug. Clumsy only because it is difficult for Jack to move with all the wires attached to his slight body. After her shift, Jack watches outside his window as Tax Law climbs into the truck and revs up the engine. Jack smiles, guessing this is her first time in a full pull.

A small tear visits Jack's right eye like a long-lost relative. Outside, it is a cloudy, somewhat foggy day. Oddly enough, however, across the endless stretch of parking lot Jack sees sun-kissed vehicles, 12 of them, all bearing the words Jesus Trucking Company, or the initials J T C.

As he blurrily examines the scene, Jack sees Max, his old college roommate. He's sitting in the cab of a 1978 GMC Sierra 6000 Stake Truck. His nine-year-old son Brent sits beside his father, a smile stretched from ear to ear.

And Willie from Denver. He's driving a 1981 Dodge D150 pickup, 6 cylinders.

Over there is the rich, crippled man from Iowa, and in the truck next to him, the poorer one, from upper Michigan. They're behind the steering wheels of twin 1986 AMC Jeep Flightline Tractors. Sitting next to the Yooper is a beautiful young lady named Amy.

There's the prison psychologist. He's got a 1984 Chevrolet Blazer, 6.2 diesel engine, automatic transmission. Examining closely, Jack detects the look of truth in his eyes.

And George and Lyman and the man who used to wear the K-Mart cap. Lyman drives a newer, though smaller truck. It looks to be a Ford. George, he has the same old Ryder, but it's transformed by a glistening new paint job.

And Juan behind them. In a 1989 Mitsubishi 4 cylinder.

Tax Law is third in the convoy, just behind Jay. That's right, Jack sees Jay, sitting comfortably in his cab. Wearing a smile and a clean heart. He's in a re-built 6-cylinder Nissan diesel, and it's just been through the wash. Soapy water drips onto asphalt like Ivory tears. Sharing Jay's cab is Janie and Dorothia, together again, forever.

Leading the team is Randi. She drives the old white Chevy pickup, the one in which she was born, the one formerly driven by her mother, Tinku. Jack bets its odometer has turned over. Twice. Randi. Jack was there for both her births.

He watches as they all back out onto the road, and drive off. He smiles at the evangelical thought that in each of us is a little of all of us—and a lot of the Lord. And Jack thanks Him, glorifies Him for the work He has done with the twelve. And, of course, with himself.

Jack's roommate Robert turns to him and through his oxygen mask utters the first words Jack has ever heard him say. "They drive on," Robert says, though the ventilator chugs away on high. "They drive on." Robert's voice sounds strange to Jack, like the muted sound a swimmer hears underwater.

"Yes, Robert, they drive on," Jack echoes, letting the remark trail off.

And Jack watches the 12 outside his room window, led by Randi, born on the shoulder of some hot, anonymous rural highway

Driving Home

in South Dakota.

Drizzle churns from the opaque sky as they pull away, one by one, a fine spring mist lasting just long enough to rainbow the oil on the long road before them, glisten the trees, ripen the fruit they carry. Puddles form where the road is uneven. Eventually, Jack's focus switches briefly from the fleet of trucks to the cross in the window—reminding him of the day, years ago, when he gave his life, completely, to Him—then back again to the fleet. To the 12. And he watches as they drive on, the rain dropping in a glassy, horizontal weft, the spirit of God bonding them once they hit the road, and—like Jack—leaving them only their love of Jesus for fuel.

"Then Jesus went around from village to village. Calling the Twelve to him, he sent them out two by two and gave them authority over evil spirits.

These were his instructions: 'Take nothing for the journey except a staff--no bread, no bag, no money in your belts. Wear sandals but not an extra tunic.

Whenever you enter a house, stay there until you leave that town. And if any place will not welcome you or listen to you, shake the dust off your feet when you leave, as a testimony against them.'"

--Mark 6:7-11